***As Careful as a Pair of Cats Sneaking Up
on a Bird, Jimmy and I Crept Along
Toward the Corner.***

We made a wide arc, away from the brick wall, and when we were where we could see our side yard, there was Mama flashing pictures as fast as she could, and Daddy shooting video film. He was smiling so hard you could see his grin on either side of the camera, and . . .

and standing between them was the most beautiful horse I had ever seen.

It was a pinto—mostly white with some big, brown spots.

"Look what Santa left," Daddy called.

"Well?" Mama stopped shooting pictures. "What do you think of him?"

Jimmy and I stood with our mouths gaping open.

It was the best Christmas present ever!

Books by Bill Wallace

Red Dog
Trapped in Death Cave

Available from ARCHWAY Paperbacks

The Backward Bird Dog
Beauty
The Biggest Klutz in Fifth Grade
Blackwater Swamp
Buffalo Gal
The Christmas Spurs
Danger in Quicksand Swamp
Danger on Panther Peak
  (Original title: Shadow on the Snow)
A Dog Called Kitty
Ferret in the Bedroom, Lizards in the Fridge
The Final Freedom
Journey into Terror
Never Say Quit
Snot Stew
Totally Disgusting!
True Friends
Upchuck and the Rotten Willy
Upchuck and the Rotten Willy: The Great Escape
Watchdog and the Coyotes

Available from MINSTREL Books

BILL WALLACE

A MINSTREL® BOOK

PUBLISHED BY POCKET BOOKS

New York   London   Toronto   Sydney   Tokyo   Singapore

With LOVE to
Noah and Joel,
Linda and Jason

 A Minstrel Book published by
POCKET BOOKS, a division of Simon & Schuster Inc.
1230 Avenue of the Americas, New York, NY 10020

Copyright © 1990 by Bill Wallace

Published by arrangement with Holiday House, Inc.

ISBN: 0-671-74505-0

First Minstrel Books printing December 1991

10 9 8 7 6

A MINSTREL BOOK and colophon are registered trademarks of Simon & Schuster Inc.

Cover art by Tom Galasinski

Printed in the U.S.A.

CHAPTER
1

I didn't like being left alone. That's the only reason I went with Mama and Daddy and Jimmy instead of staying home or going over to play football with David Beckman. Well that, and because they told me I *had* to go.

Daddy didn't like driving in the Oklahoma City rush-hour traffic. He said it made him nervous. When Daddy was nervous, Mama and I were nervous, too.

Jimmy wasn't nervous though. He was in the backseat with me. He had his hand stuck out the open window behind Mama. He waved it up and down against the rushing wind, making noises like an airplane.

I figured Jimmy ought to be nervous about Daddy having to drive in the rush-hour traffic. After all, it was his doctor's appointment at nine that got us into this mess. I mean, if it weren't for him, I could be home playing with my friends.

Besides, I remember when I was Jimmy's age. Mama and Daddy wouldn't let me stick my hand out the window.

"Jimmy's got his hand out the window," I said.

Mama glanced over her shoulder. "Get your hand inside," she said. Only, as soon as she turned around, Jimmy stuck it back out in the warm August wind that rushed past our car.

He started giggling. When Jimmy giggled, it sounded like tiny bells jingling inside a tin bucket. His giggle was so high and shrill, it made the hair prickle on the back of my neck.

I frowned, wondering why Mama and Daddy didn't give him the lecture about a truck or bus coming along and knocking his arm off. They always made *me* get my arm in.

With Jimmy, it was different. Nobody yelled at him. He got to do a lot of stuff I never got to. When I asked about it, Mama and Daddy always told me it was because I was the oldest and they expected more out of me. That didn't explain anything though.

It made me mad. "Get your arm in the car," I told him. "You'll get it knocked off."

Jimmy kind of stuck his nose up at me and kept right on playing like his hand was an airplane. His shrill, squeaky giggle made my lip curl. I punched him on the shoulder.

"Mama, Nick hit me," he whined in his highest voice.

"He's got his hand out the window," I said.

Mama ignored both of us.

"Look over there." She pointed to a big open field. "That's where the new shopping mall is going to be."

"They're coming right along with it," Daddy said.

"Watch where you're going, you idiot!" he yelled, shaking his fist at the little blue car that shot in front of us to get to the exit. "You dumb . . ." Then he mumbled something that I couldn't hear.

I glanced out the window where Mama pointed. There were a whole bunch of earthmovers and big machines. They were as busy as ants, pushing the grass and trees away. They were making the hills flat and filling in the valleys. The red, Oklahoma dust swirled around them like a tornado.

After hearing about the mall on the news and after hearing Daddy read about it out loud from the newspaper, it was hard to believe that this flat dusty field was all there was.

But when the workmen finished, USA Central Mall in Oklahoma City would be the biggest shopping mall in the whole, entire world. Even bigger than anything in Texas. Daddy said that this was "really" important to some people in Oklahoma, because they were always trying to outdo Texas in something. He laughed because he said that Texas was more than twice as big as we were and it had more than three times as many people and the folks who ran their state government had more sense than our guys did—although not much.

Anyway, the mall was going to open the day after Thanksgiving. Mama always reminded us that that was *next* Thanksgiving, not this one. It was going to be four stories tall and there would be an ice-skating rink (bigger than the one at the Galleria in Dallas or Houston) *and* a roller-skating rink, too.

There were going to be all sorts of stores: Neiman Marcus, Saks Fifth Avenue, FAO Schwartz, J. C. Penney, Ward's, Sears, even a Gucchi's and a Tiffany's.

Altogether, there would be over seven hundred shops when the mall was finished, and it would cover over one square mile of Oklahoma City.

To me, it looked just like a big, dirty field.

When we passed it, Jimmy turned around in the seat and stuck his head out the window. I grabbed his belt.

"Mama, Jimmy's hanging out of the car again."

Mama got up on her knees in the front seat and turned around to help me pull him back in. Then, she pointed beside her.

"Right up here, young man. If you can't behave, you'll just have to sit where I can watch you."

As usual, when Jimmy climbed over the front seat, he clunked Daddy upside the head with his tennis shoe. Daddy rubbed his ear and mumbled something, but he never took his eyes off his driving. I guess he was used to getting kicked when one of us climbed over the seat.

"Are they gonna have machines like that when they do the church?" Jimmy wondered.

Mama shook her head.

"No. They're just remodeling the church, adding on a Sunday-school section and a recreation room for the kids. I don't think they'll need all those machines." She leaned around Jimmy to look at Daddy. "You tell Reverend Parks that you wouldn't be there to help today?"

Daddy grunted and nodded his head.

"They've got plenty of carpenters. Besides, he won't even need me until they get finished with the foundation work. He did give me a couple of phone numbers to call—if I have time. I'm supposed to check on new speakers for the chapel. That old speaker is starting to make weird noises. Time to get rid of it and get a new system."

When we pulled off the six-lane at the exit, we had to stop for a light at the bottom of the ramp. Once the car stopped and the wind quit rushing by, I could feel the heat. Even this early in the morning, Oklahoma's hot in August.

I wished the light would change so we could get moving again. Daddy wished it would, too.

"Oklahoma City's got the longest lights in the country," he snarled. "Sit here till we turn gray-headed. Are they trying to set a record for long lights or something?"

Mama reached across Jimmy. "Want me to turn the air conditioner on?"

"No. We're almost there."

I remember thinking, as we drove up to Children's Memorial Hospital, that if the shopping mall we passed was as big as this place, it really *would* be the biggest mall in the world.

When Daddy parked the car in the huge, cold, cement parking garage with all the cold metal cars everywhere around us, Jimmy reached over and tugged at my sleeve.

"I'm scared," he said.

CHAPTER
2

We took the elevator down to the ground floor. Daddy let Jimmy push the button, but he told me I could push it when we came back.

We walked across a big, open, cement yard toward a tall brick building that didn't have any windows. My mouth opened when I leaned my head back to look up at it.

Two men with uniforms stood near the door. They looked at everybody who walked past. Their stares were mean and angry.

We walked through a big lobby with statues and a small fountain that gargled and bubbled. Then we found another elevator and went up. There was a whole bunch of people on it, so neither Jimmy nor I got to push the buttons.

We went down a long hall with lots of doors. There were

people in white coats and women in white uniforms with white shoes that squeaked when they walked. We went down another long hallway. Then we crossed a big sidewalk covered on the top and sides with glass that took us from one big building to an even bigger building. We got lost and Daddy grumped and fussed and Mama finally found a map thing on the wall. So we went down some more long halls with lots of doors, took the elevator up one more floor, and found the office with the people who were going to look at Jimmy. We sat in big chairs next to the wall for a long, long time—with nothing to do.

Jimmy kept holding my hand. His feet wiggled because they didn't touch the floor. My feet touched the floor, but they wiggled, too.

Finally, a lady in a white uniform and squeaky shoes came over.

"Jimmy Tipton?"

Mama got up. Daddy got up. Jimmy and I didn't.

"Yes, ma'am," Mama answered the lady. Then she smiled down at me. "We'll be just a minute or two with the doctor. If it's going to take very long, Daddy or I will come back to stay with you. You be all right?"

I made my chest puff out. "Sure. I'll be fine. I'll just read a magazine."

She reached down for Jimmy's hand. Only, he kept holding on to me and wouldn't let go.

"I'm scared," he whispered in my ear. "I don't wanna go."

I was scared, too. I didn't want to be left alone. I didn't want Jimmy to go. Only, when you're a big brother, you can't be scared. Big brothers have to be brave.

I squeezed his hand, then reached down and pried his fingers loose.

"Quit being such a baby," I said. "There isn't anything to be scared of. Go on with Mama."

Jimmy let go and they left.

I was sure glad to see Daddy.

I had been alone for an awfully long time, and there'd been nothing to do. I looked at some of the pictures in the magazine, but the words were too hard to read. One of the nurses asked me if I wanted a piece of candy, but I didn't. A little girl who was waiting with her mama and daddy played peep-eye with me for a while. It was kind of fun, but she was too little to talk with and after a while she had to go see the doctor, too.

Daddy reached down and ruffled my hair.

"Let's go get a Coke or go to a show. They're going to be in there for a while."

I smoothed my hair down with my fingers.

"I want to wait for Jimmy," I said. "You could read to me."

Daddy sat in the chair next to mine. He patted my leg.

"Jimmy has to go through a whole bunch of tests. Mama's going to stay with him. It's gonna take all day, and there's no sense in us trying to stay here with nothing to do. Come on."

I got up, but I didn't want to leave without Jimmy.

Daddy smiled down at me, but his eyes were worried.

"You want to see a movie?"

I shook my head.

"How about getting something to eat?"

I shook my head.

"Want to go to Crossroads Mall and see if we can find some toys?"

I shook my head.

Daddy shot a blast of air up his forehead. It made his hair bounce. Then he looked at me and lifted his eyebrows.

"How about stopping by a Seven-Eleven and getting a pop and some chips? I could use the pay phone and call those companies about the speaker systems for Reverend Parks. Then we could go over to where they're building the new mall and watch the big machines."

I smiled and nodded my head.

Next to watching cowboy shows or playing cowboys in the backyard, Jimmy liked watching big machines best. I could tell him all about the machines when he got through at the doctor's.

CHAPTER

3

By the time Jimmy got through at the doctor's, it was rush hour again. Only this time, Daddy didn't fuss at the other drivers. He didn't yell and shake his fist. He didn't even mumble stuff that I couldn't understand. He just drove the car. He and Mama didn't say a word.

Afternoon rush hour was even worse than in the morning. The cars were packed together almost as close as we had been in the parking garage. Daddy had to drive so slowly that Jimmy couldn't stick his hand out the window and play airplane in the wind.

Jimmy finally got bored. He lay down in the seat and put his head in my lap. Usually when he did this, I shoved him off and told him to stay on his own side of the car.

This time I didn't.

12

He almost always flopped and wiggled around a lot. But now, his head just stayed in one spot—real tiredlike. There were little Band-Aids on his arms, and he went right to sleep without even squirming.

We hadn't driven far on the four-lane when Daddy asked Mama if she wanted to eat at Applewoods.

I liked Applewoods. It was a fun place to eat. From the time we'd get there until the food came, this lady would come around with a basket and put apple fritters on our plates. They were fried-bread things, covered with lots of powdered sugar and with little chunks of apple inside.

"I want to go home," was all Mama said.

The way she said it scared me. Her voice cracked like she was crying. I tried to lean over and see if she had tears, only with Jimmy's head in my lap, I couldn't get far enough to see her face.

When we got to Chickasha, Daddy stopped at Hardee's. In the drive-through he and Mama got a salad. Jimmy and I got a hamburger and fries and everybody got a shake. We went home to eat.

I was still worried about Mama because she didn't talk much or eat much of her salad. She only played with it. Mama didn't have any tears though.

When we finished, Mama went to her room. She said she was going to take a nap. Daddy went out to mow the yard.

Now, I was really getting worried. Mama never took a nap. Daddy never mowed the lawn this late in the evening. Besides, he just mowed it last week.

Something was wrong, and nobody would tell me what.

Jimmy blew some more bubbles in his shake, then finished slurping the foam off the bottom of the cup. I took our trash and put it in the can in the kitchen. We went outside to play on the tire swing in the backyard.

I shoved Jimmy—trying to keep the tire straight so it wouldn't spin around and around.

"What did the doctor say?" I asked when I shoved.

"Nothing," he answered, swooping back to me.

"Nothing?"

"Nothing."

I shoved again.

"Are you sick?"

He swung to me.

"I don't know."

I shoved it again.

"Do you have to go again?"

He swung back to me.

"I don't know."

This time, instead of shoving him, I caught the tire.

"Were you in there, right before we went home, with Mama and Daddy?"

"Yes."

"Was the doctor with you?"

"Yes."

"Did he talk to Mama and Daddy?"

"Yes."

"Well . . . what did he say?"

There was a long pause.

"I don't know."

I ground my teeth together. Little brothers sure are dumb sometimes.

"Look," I said, turning the tire so he had to face me, "you were in there. The doctor was in there. And he was talking to Mama and Daddy. Surely you heard them talking."

Jimmy shrugged.

"Yeah. But they were using big words and talking soft and I don't know what they were talking about. I couldn't understand the words."

My shoulders sagged. I think grown-ups talk like that when they don't want kids to know what's going on. I started shoving Jimmy's tire again.

I got him going real fast before pushing on one side of the tire, as hard as I could. He spun round and round and round. Jimmy squealed and laughed—that high, squeaky laugh that sounded like tiny bells jingling in a tin bucket.

After that, we played catch with the Nerf soccer ball. Jimmy told me about the needles they poked him with and all the blood they took out of his arm and about a big, cold table he had to lie on so they could take something called X rays and about a thing like a cave that they put him in. He said the table they made him lie on slid right into the cave. There were lights on the walls of the cave and it made a loud, roaring noise and it went in a circle around him. He wanted to take off running and get out of the cave, but the nurses told him to lie very, very still and not to move. He said they made it sound awfully important and scary, so even though he was so scared he wanted to run, he didn't.

"I felt like, if I tried to run, the cave monster or something was gonna get me."

He laughed when he said that. I laughed, too.

We talked some more and I told him about Daddy and me going to watch the big machines at the new mall. I told him about the huge thing with big tires that looked like a truck, only it had blades on the bottom that scooped up the dirt as it drove across the top of a hill. There were a bunch of machines like that, and they would take the dirt and dump it beside the creeks or gullies, before bulldozers would shove it into the low spots and drive back and forth over it to pack it down.

Then we decided to go in and watch John Wayne and *The Cowboys* on the VCR. While Jimmy was finding the right tape, I glanced out the front window to see how Daddy was doing with the lawn.

He screwed the gas cap back on the mower and set the gas can on the driveway. He tugged on the starter rope a couple of times. It didn't start.

He fiddled with something on the side of the mower, then pulled the rope a couple more times. It still didn't start.

I knew what was coming next.

Only . . . what was supposed to happen didn't happen. Daddy didn't kick the lawn mower. He didn't yell at it. He didn't call it bad names that made Mama's face turn red or made her put her hands over our ears.

He didn't do *anything*.

Instead, he plopped down on his bottom, right in the middle of the front yard. He put his face in his hands and just sat there.

I *knew* something was wrong. Now I was really scared—scared more than I could ever remember. But, as I said, when you're a big brother, you can't be scared. So I went in and watched *The Cowboys* with Jimmy.

About halfway through the movie, Jimmy had to go to the bathroom. I went in the kitchen where Mama was. I walked right up to her and put my hands on my hips.

"What's wrong with Jimmy?" I demanded.

Mama reached out and hugged me tight against her. I thought she was crying because of the way her tummy jerked, only I couldn't see any tears.

"Nothing," she managed.

Daddy came in about then. He was all dusty and grungy from mowing the dirt (there wasn't much grass to mow). I turned to him.

"What's wrong with Jimmy?"

He ruffled my hair and looked at Mama.

"Nothing."

Something was wrong. Bad wrong. And since nobody would tell me what, I was going to find out for myself.

CHAPTER
4

Little brothers are such a pain!

Sometimes, when Jimmy had trouble sleeping, I'd lie in his room until he dozed off. But tonight, Jimmy wouldn't go to sleep. He flipped and flopped and twisted and turned. He wanted me to read him a bedtime story. He wanted a drink of water. He wanted to clunk me over the head with his pillow, but I told him if he did, I'd punch him right in the mouth.

Finally, he settled down.

When I was pretty sure he was asleep, I eased out of his bed without making a sound. Quiet as could be, I crept down the hall. It was a trick I discovered when I was little. Whenever Mama and Daddy had a fight (they always called it a "discussion"), I'd sneak out of my room and go stand outside their room—just to hear if they were still fighting or if they'd made up. I held my breath and leaned my ear, very gently, against their door.

They were quiet—already asleep.

Darn ol' Jimmy, I thought. If he had shut up earlier, I could have reached Mama and Daddy's room in time to listen to what they were saying. Now, I'd have to wait. But, somehow, I'd find out what was wrong.

Only, every time I asked, they just said, "Nothing."

Mama and Daddy seemed happier for the next few days. Then, on Friday, we went to Oklahoma City again. Jimmy had to go see a different doctor at a different hospital, for what Mama and Daddy called "a second opinion"— whatever that is.

We spent the whole day there and when we were finished, Mama and Daddy took us to a show and out to eat at Applewoods before we drove home.

After seeing the second doctor though, Mama and Daddy weren't happy anymore. Mama cried on the drive home, real tears that she couldn't hold back.

Jimmy didn't say much. Mama, Daddy, and the doctor used big words again that a little kid like him couldn't understand. He did say that he was tired and he didn't like being poked with needles and he was scared.

I was scared, too, only I didn't let on.

I was sorry that Jimmy was scared, but I was glad that he was tired. That meant he would go to sleep right away and

I could try sneaking down to listen to Mama and Daddy again.

Jimmy slept all the way home, so when we got there, he was wide awake and wanted me to read a book to him.

"I'm tired," I said. "I want to go to bed."

"I wanna hear you read a book," he pouted.

"You've had a long day. Let's go to sleep," I answered.

He folded his arms and pouched out his bottom lip.

I sighed. "All right. How about *The Blind Colt*?"

Jimmy didn't listen to *The Blind Colt* though. He sat there, staring up at the ceiling, but he didn't listen. He just looked off into space with kind of a blank stare, and didn't even smile at the funny parts.

"What's wrong?" I asked finally.

Jimmy leaned toward me. His voice was almost a whisper.

"I think I'm real bad sick," he said. "Only I don't know. Nobody will tell me. I heard them say I'd have to go back to the doctor's for 'treatments,' but I don't know what they are."

He glanced around, like he was making sure nobody else was listening.

"It's not fair! I mean . . . I'm the one who's got something wrong with him, and I don't know what it is. Everybody else knows. But I don't. It's not fair."

I shrugged.

"I don't know either, Jimmy. You're not the only one. Maybe there's nothing wrong with you. Or maybe there *is* something wrong and Mama and Daddy figure you don't want to know what it is."

"I *do* want to know, Nick."

"Are you sure?"

He made a gulping sound as he swallowed.

"I'm sure."

I reached over and patted his leg. Then I got up from the couch. "Come on. We'll go ask them. Maybe if both of us . . ."

He got up and followed me to the kitchen. Mama was drying the dishes. Daddy was reading the paper.

"We want to know what's wrong with Jimmy," I announced in my bravest voice.

Mama's eyes were red. She glanced at us, then turned around and dried the plate she was working on and put it away. Daddy peeked over the top of his paper.

"What makes you think there's something wrong?"

I folded my arms, trying to look grown-up.

"We've made two trips to the doctors in Oklahoma City. Mama cried both times. You didn't cuss at the dumb drivers when we drove home, then you mowed the grass when there wasn't any grass and . . ."

"And Mama keeps drying dishes that she's already dried," Jimmy cut in.

Mama's shoulders sagged. She put her elbows on the counter by the sink and buried her face in the dish towel. Daddy folded the paper and put it beside his coffee cup.

Jimmy and I sat down at our places on either side of him.

"I think you ought to tell us. Jimmy wants to know, and if he's the one that's sick you ought to tell him. I want to know, too, 'cause he's my brother and it's not fair that we don't know what's going on."

Daddy took a deep breath. "Terri . . ." he said to Mama. "Come sit down. We . . . ah . . . er," he stammered. "We all need to talk. . . . I guess. . . ."

Mama wiped her face with the dish towel. She came and sat at the other end of the table from Daddy.

Daddy took a big drink of his coffee. Then he kind of chewed at the inside of his lip—so hard that it made his mouth scrunch up at one side.

"Jimmy's very sick, very sick," he began slowly. "The doctors say he'll have to go back over to Oklahoma City a whole bunch of times for treatments . . . and . . ."

"What're treatments?" Jimmy interrupted.

"They're medicine to help fight the disease you have," Mama answered.

"Why can't he take medicine at home?" I wondered. "We have lots of pills and stuff for when we get sick. Why does he have to go to Oklahoma City?"

Daddy patted my arm.

"The medicine they have to give him doesn't come in pills. They have to . . ."

"I don't like shots," Jimmy whined. "They hurt."

Mama pushed the dish towel over her face again.

"It's not really shots either," Daddy said. "Well . . . yeah, I guess it is kind of like a shot. You remember when they took blood out of your arm?" he asked Jimmy.

Jimmy nodded.

Daddy tried to smile. "It's kind of like that, only when they put the needle in the vein, instead of taking blood out, they're gonna be putting medicine in."

Jimmy rubbed at the little, round Band-Aid over the crease where his arm bent.

"Will the medicine hurt?"

Daddy shrugged.

"I honestly don't know. The doctors didn't tell us if it would hurt or not. They did say that it makes some people sick. They said that some people lose their hair. But they never said if it hurts or not."

"I don't want it to hurt." Jimmy pouted.

I kicked him under the table—not hard, just enough to get him to listen.

"If it hurts a little, that's okay. You're tough. If it makes you better, it doesn't matter."

Then, a bad feeling kind of swept over me. I felt a chill run up the back of my neck. I turned to Daddy.

"Will it make him better?"

Daddy didn't answer. He squeezed his eyes shut, real tight. It didn't help though, because two tears slipped out anyway and rolled down his cheek. Mama put her dish towel in her lap. She reached over and took my hand, and with the other, she took Jimmy's.

She swallowed hard. Then, not looking at us, but at our hands that she held so tightly, she said:

"Jimmy has leukemia."

CHAPTER

5

That night, I tried not to think about it. I tried to shut my eyes and sleep, only the sleep wouldn't come.

It wasn't the word "leukemia" that bothered me. Neither Jimmy nor I really knew what it meant. It was the way Mama had said it. The way her voice cracked. The way more tears leaked from Daddy's eyes and the quick way he got up to go out and "work" in the garage.

I flopped on my other side. I rolled my tongue over in my mouth and chewed on it. Not hard, just enough to feel the pressure.

"Lots of people can't roll their tongue upside down," Mama had told me once. "It's a trait you inherited from your daddy."

I bit down on my tongue.

I wondered if leukemia was something I would inherit from Jimmy.

At night, Jimmy and I left our bedroom doors open all the time, unless we got in trouble for fighting. Then Mama made us close them.

There was a faint sound from his room. I propped myself up on my elbows and leaned toward Jimmy's room, listening.

I frowned at the sniffing sound I heard.

"You all right, Jimmy?" I called softly so as not to bother Mama and Daddy.

He sniffed again. "I'm scared, Nick."

A tear slipped from my eye. I wiped it on my shoulder and clamped my jaws tight so I wouldn't make crying noises when I answered him.

"There's nothing to be scared about. You're gonna be all right. Mama said that the doctors told her that sixty percent of the people with your kind of leukemia get over it."

"What does that mean?" His bed squeaked when he sat up.

"Well . . . we studied percent stuff in school. It means that out of every hundred people who get it, sixty get over it."

There was a long silence. Then Jimmy's bed squeaked again.

"What happens to the other forty?"

I bit down on my lip. It hurt. No matter, I bit down even

harder. It was the question I was afraid he was going to ask.

"I don't know," I lied, fighting back the tears.

Jimmy flipped his light on. I moved my elbows in the blink of an eye and flopped down on the bed, hoping the pillow would hide my tears from him.

"Will my hair fall out?"

I bit the pillow as hard as I could, then swallowed.

"I don't know, Jimmy. I do know we have to take you to the doctor in Oklahoma City tomorrow to start your treatments. You need your rest." And as bravely as I could sound, I added, "Now shut up and go to sleep!"

He turned his light off.

I wrapped the pillow around my face so he wouldn't hear me sniffling.

I didn't want to tell Jimmy to shut up and go to sleep. But, when you're a big brother—when you're mostly grown up—you don't cry, no matter how scared you are. Besides, if I let on to Jimmy how scared I was, it would only make him feel worse. So, I squeezed the pillow tighter around my face and made myself quit shaking.

Please let him be okay. Please, God. Please don't let anything bad happen to him . . . Please. . . .

Somewhere between our crying and sniffling and prayers, Jimmy and I both fell asleep.

CHAPTER

6

"And will you tell me about all the big machines? And about the one with the tires that are bigger than a car and all the noise and . . ."

I ruffled Jimmy's hair.

"I'll tell you about all that stuff."

"Promise?"

I made an X over my chest with my finger.

"Promise."

Jimmy and Mama went with the nurse in the white uniform and squeaky shoes. Daddy and I waited until they disappeared into a doorway at the end of the hall, then we went to the parking lot and got the car.

"I wish Jimmy could see this," I said.

Daddy took a sip of his diet Dr Pepper. "Me, too," he said, patting my leg.

"He loves big machines," I told Daddy. "I bet when he grows up he's gonna drive one of those things. Like that one over there."

I pointed to the earthmover with the huge wheels. The blades underneath it scooped up enormous mouthfuls of dirt and stored them in the belly of the machine. When it was full, the machine drove to a little pond surrounded by lots of trees and let all the dirt out. Then it started back for another load of dirt.

"You think Jimmy will be a machine driver?"

Daddy didn't answer.

I glanced over at him. He was wiping his eyes.

"Are you crying, Daddy?"

He shook his head. "No," he sniffed. "Just got a bug or dust or something . . ."

I didn't bother Daddy anymore. Instead, I went back to watching the machines. Besides, I thought, maybe daddies are like big brothers. Maybe they have to be brave when they're really not. Maybe daddies can't cry when they want to. Anyway, I promised Jimmy I would tell him all about the machines. Daddy would feel better if I watched them instead of him.

I didn't get to keep my promise to Jimmy though. When Daddy and I got back that afternoon to pick up him and Mama, they weren't there.

The lady in the white uniform told us where they were though, so we went to another big building that was close by. When we got to the tenth floor, we got off the elevator and walked up to the nurse at the desk.

"Jimmy Tipton's room?" Daddy asked.

The lady thumbed through some papers on her desk. She read something, then pointed to her right.

"Down the hall through the double doors on your left. He's in Ward 1007."

Daddy smiled and nodded. We started for the hall, but before we got very far, the lady called out to stop us.

"I'm sorry," she said, "the ward is closed to everyone but parents."

Daddy put his arm around my shoulder.

"This is Jimmy's brother."

The woman shook her head.

"Again, I'm sorry," she apologized, "but there are no children allowed in the ward . . ."

"Not even brothers?"

"Not even brothers. He can stay in the waiting room by the water fountain."

I saw Daddy's forehead turn kind of red. Before he could say anything else to the lady, I tugged at his arm.

"It's okay, Daddy. I'm big enough to wait by myself. I'll be all right."

He smiled and ruffled my hair. Then, he gave a real mean look to the lady and took me to the waiting room.

The waiting room was just what the lady had said—a

waiting room. I waited and waited and waited. It wasn't much fun either.

Everything was so squeaky-clean. I was scared to touch stuff 'cause I might get something dirty. There was a TV, but the only things on it were soap operas. I found a checkerboard with most of the checkers missing, so I played a game by myself with what was there. I spotted some magazines, but they were for old folks and were nothing I could read or even wanted to read.

It was scary, too, because I was all alone and the place smelled like a hospital—which it was supposed to smell like because it *was* a hospital. There were people in the halls talking and metal stuff that clanked every once in a while—and *nothing* to do.

It took forever for Mama and Daddy to finally come and get me.

"I'm going to stay here with Jimmy," Mama said. "You and Daddy are going to go back home and . . ."

"What's wrong with Jimmy?" My voice was shaking.

Mama gave me a gentle pat on the cheek.

"Nothing's wrong with Jimmy. The medicine he had was just a little too strong for him. It made him sick."

I frowned. "How sick?"

"He's just kind of throwing up and real weak. The doctors want him to stay here a couple of days to be sure he's okay."

Mama got down on one knee. She hugged me, hard.

"I promise. He's okay. Really."

She got up and hugged Daddy. "Call Mr. Gibson when you get home. Tell him that I won't be there for teacher in-service or enrollment on Wednesday. Can you enroll Nick?"

Daddy nodded. "We'll be fine. Where are you going to stay?"

"Jimmy wants me with him. There's a big chair and . . ."

"You can't spend two nights in a chair."

Mama smiled. "I'll be fine. Jimmy needs me with him. If you could run some clean clothes over in the morning before you go to work . . ."

Daddy kissed her.

"Are you sure you'll be all right?"

Mama kissed him back.

"I'm sure. The doctors said it would take a couple of times for his system to adjust to the medication and for them to figure out the right dosage. After that, it'll just be one day every two weeks. We'll drive up in the morning and home that evening. It'll be easy after these first couple of times."

Driving home without Mama and Jimmy didn't make me feel too good. Daddy tried to talk so I'd feel better. He said that we could go fishing when Jimmy got home and that after a little while things would be back to normal.

I listened to him. Still, something inside kept gnawing at me, kept telling me that maybe things *wouldn't* be normal—not ever.

CHAPTER

7

The voice inside was the one I should have listened to. Daddy talked about everything being okay and about us going fishing and about Jimmy driving one of those big dirt-moving machines and all the fun we'd have together and how everything would be back to normal. His words weren't real. His words were what his insides hoped would happen—not what really was.

The gnawing, hurtie voice inside me had told me the truth.

Over the next three months, Jimmy never did get used to the medicine. Every time we took him to the city, he had to stay at least three days, sometimes the whole week. We never knew how long it was going to be.

The medicine was hard on Jimmy and spending the

nights at the hospital was hard on Mama. After the first couple of times, she would take an overnight bag and a change of clothes. One night, when Mama and Daddy didn't know I was listening, I snuck down to their room. Mama was telling Daddy about the plastic-covered chair and how, just about the time she got comfortable, she'd slide out of the thing.

She tried to laugh, only I could tell she was really tired when she'd get home from one of their stays. Daddy said she ought to get a motel room, but Mama said that Jimmy was scared and needed her there. "Besides," she'd added, "even with our insurance, this is going to cost a fortune. We can't afford any more expenses."

When Mama and Jimmy did get to come home, between visits to the hospital, Jimmy wasn't Jimmy.

Well . . . sometimes he was . . . but not always.

Most of the time he was real tired and weak and he didn't want to play. When I'd tell him about the machines and about how they had started building one of the walls for the new mall, he'd try to listen, but lots of times, he'd fall asleep.

I remember telling him about the pretty little pond with big trees around it and how bulldozers knocked the trees down and filled the pond with dirt. He stayed awake while I told him about that. When I finished, I remember him saying something about how it was kind of sad.

"I think those big machines are really neat," he said, "but it's too bad that they had to take down the trees and fill up the pond. Because when there are no trees and no ponds, the birds don't have a place to live and they go away and that's one thing I really miss when I'm in the hospital—I don't get to see or listen to birds and stuff."

It made me feel kind of sad, too.

During that time, the doctors managed to move things around so Mama and Jimmy could go to the hospital on Sunday afternoons. That way, Daddy and I could take them, and Daddy didn't have to miss work on Monday mornings. We never knew for sure, though, when Jimmy would get to come home. Sometimes, the medicine would make him sick, and instead of picking them up on Monday afternoons, we would have to wait clear up until Wednesday.

Usually, Jimmy was home on weekends. That meant we could watch Saturday morning cartoons and play some, if he felt like it. He hardly ever felt like it though.

On Sunday mornings, we would go to the First Christian Church. It was near downtown, on Kansas and Sixth streets. During those three months, we went to Sunday school and church every week.

Before, we didn't go every Sunday. Sometimes I would fuss about having to put dress-up clothes on. And sometimes I would get Daddy interested in the cowboy movie that came on Channel 25 at about nine. Or sometimes I'd just sleep late and beg them not to get me up and make me get dressed.

But now that Jimmy was so sick, for some reason I didn't

mind going at all. I liked listening to Mrs. Wineham play the organ. Even though it was old and one of the deep, bass notes sometimes made a little rumbling sound, Mrs. Wineham played it well.

I always sat in the balcony because I remembered that when I was little, the preacher had once talked about God and the angels. I had leaned over and asked Mama where the angels were. She had pointed to the top of the church. "Up there," she'd said. "Now be quiet."

I was about five or so, I guess—about Jimmy's age. I expected to see the angels sitting on the big, wooden beams that stretched across the top of the chapel.

I remember being a little disappointed when I didn't see them.

There was a big speaker above the choir and the communion table at the front of the church. The speaker was up high—even higher than the rafters. The front was covered with brown cloth and it was made of brown wood. The thing was bigger than I was and the sound of Reverend Parks's voice came from it when he talked into the microphone.

I remembered him talking about how this was God's house, and how God was always with us—even if we couldn't see Him.

And I remember thinking to myself that the big speaker box looked like the lectern where the preacher stood. If God really was here, He'd probably be sittin' right there on that speaker. He'd be looking down at all the people and listening to their prayers.

Only, since He was God, we couldn't see Him.

When you're little, you do dumb things—you think dumb thoughts. But now that I was mostly grown-up, it didn't matter. So what if there weren't any angels up here on the rafters? So what if I couldn't see God sitting on the big speaker or standing behind it? It didn't matter—because being up here, I *felt* like I was a little closer to God. And, maybe if I was closer, He might hear my prayers a tiny bit better. Maybe he would listen when I talked to Him about helping Jimmy.

Anyway, I always asked Mama and Daddy if I could sit in the balcony.

Jimmy was supposed to start kindergarten that year, only he didn't. Mama and Daddy decided it would be best if he waited until next year. Mama got a year's leave of absence from her job as second-grade teacher. That meant she didn't get fired or anything. It meant that she could take a year off to help Jimmy and then have her job back next year.

Daddy kept going to work, and when Mama and Jimmy had to stay extra days at the hospital, I spent a lot of time after school with David Beckman and his family. David was my best friend at school, but his house was clear across town.

I liked David a bunch. His mom and dad were nice, too. Only, nice as they were, I would have much rather had Mama and Jimmy home so I could be with them.

At Christmastime, our fourth-grade teacher, Mrs. Ohl, read us *The Littlest Angel*.

I cried.

None of the other guys did, but I did.

It embarrassed me—a little. But nobody made fun of me. Mrs. Ohl knew what was wrong with Jimmy and so did everybody else in the class. I guess that's why nobody teased me about crying.

The week before Christmas vacation, Mrs. Ohl asked us to write a letter to Santa. She said the newspaper would print some of them.

At recess, everybody ran around asking one another what presents they were going to list in their letters. I wanted a real pair of cowboy spurs, the kind with a star that jingled. And I wanted a basketball and a BB gun and some new Westerns to read to Jimmy. (It was awfully hard to find good Western kids' books.) And I wanted some new Nintendo games and a gillion-and-one neat toys I had seen on TV.

That afternoon, when we worked on our letters, I wrote down all the stuff I could think of. Right before we turned them in, Mrs. Ohl said, "Don't get too carried away. Just put down what you really want because the paper won't print them if they're too long. Remember—just what you really want."

I think she was talking to Tina Simpkin because she was already starting on the third page of her list. But no matter who she was talking to, I listened. I looked down at all the stuff on my paper and I thought about what I *really* wanted.

And when I thought about what I really wanted, I got out another sheet from my notebook. I just wrote one sentence on it. That's the one that came out in the newspaper.

I want my brother and my mama back.

Nick Tipton

CHAPTER
8

It was the first time since second grade that I really and truly believed in Santa Claus.

The Sunday that my letter appeared in the newspaper, Mama had to take Jimmy back to the doctor. Only instead of having to stay three or four days, they called us to come and get them that very evening.

"Jimmy's leukemia is in remission," Mama announced the second Daddy and I got there.

Daddy swooped her up in his arms and spun her around and around. They laughed and cried and hollered and giggled and leaped about—all at once. The people who walked in and out of the hospital looked at us kind of funny.

Jimmy was on the other side of where they were dancing up and down. He leaned around and smiled at me. I smiled back and stuck my thumb up. He did, too.

When Mama and Daddy finally settled down, I asked them what "remission" was and how Jimmy's sickness got "in it."

Before Mama answered, she and Daddy grabbed me and Jimmy and all four of us had a big hug. Then she said that remission meant that the leukemia had quit acting up. Leukemia was a cancer that grew in a person's blood. It killed off the good blood and left cancer that wasn't any good. She said that Jimmy's cancer had stopped growing.

When I asked if that meant Jimmy was well, Mama and Daddy hugged us again. They didn't answer my question though. That worried me all the way home.

Once we were home, I didn't stay worried very long, I guess. And on Christmas morning, Jimmy and I were both so excited that we didn't have time to worry about anything.

"You awake yet?" he called from his bed.

It was the third time he had asked me if I was awake. He knew good and well I was awake, but he kept asking anyway—each time, just a little louder than before— figuring sooner or later Mama and Daddy would hear him.

We both lay still for a minute, listening for their voices. No sound came from down the hall.

"I've had it," Jimmy said as he swung his feet over the side of the bed. "Let's go get 'em."

I jumped up and followed him down the hall. From Mama and Daddy's door, it was only about a step or two to the living room. In fact, you didn't even have to take a step. You could lean way out and see around the corner. You could see the Christmas tree and all the presents and everything.

It was sure hard, but neither one of us peeked.

Mama and Daddy were still asleep. (They always slept late on Christmas morning.) I jumped in between them on the king-sized bed. Jimmy climbed over Daddy. When he did, he stuck his knee right in the middle of Daddy's stomach.

Daddy made a loud grunting sound and sat straight up in bed. "What the . . ." he said, his eyes flashing wide open.

Jimmy was tickled by the startled look on Daddy's face and started giggling. I laughed, too. Mama rolled over and yawned. She lifted the covers so Jimmy and I could crawl underneath.

It felt good to be in bed with Mama and Daddy. It felt nice to have all four of us together.

"Can we go see what Santa brought?" Jimmy asked. "Can we? Can we?"

Daddy rubbed the spot where Jimmy had pounced on his stomach.

"Just a minute. Let me wake up, first," he said, yawning.

"Can we just go peek?" Jimmy pleaded. "We won't open anything. Just one little peek, huh?"

Daddy wrapped the pillow around his head.

"Please, Daddy? Just one peek. Please?"

"Just a minute," Daddy moaned. "What time is it any-way?"

"Seven-thirty," I answered, looking at the bright red numbers on the radio alarm beside the dresser.

He yawned again. "That's too early."

"It's Christmas morning," Jimmy and I both answered at the very same time.

Daddy's eyes kind of twinkled. He moaned, kicked the covers back, and slung his feet over the side of the bed. Mama got out on the other side. Jimmy and I lay perfectly still. Mama and Daddy bumped into each other as they started through the door. Mama patted Daddy on the seat. Jimmy giggled.

It would take a few minutes for Daddy to get the video camera ready and for the flash on Mama's camera to get warmed up. They always liked to take pictures when we first came in and saw all the neat stuff under the tree. It was kind of a Christmas morning ritual at our house, and we knew that if we bolted for the door before they called us, it would only take twice as long for them to get ready.

Waiting is not something anyone likes to do. On Christmas, though, it's harder than at any other time. We waited and waited and waited.

Nobody called.

"You reckon the camera broke?" Jimmy wondered.

I shook my head. "No, if the camera was broken, Daddy would be talking to it like he talks to the lawn mower. And we could hear that!"

Jimmy nodded.

"We sure could."

We sat quietly for a while, wondering why no one had called us to come open our presents. Finally, Jimmy pushed the covers back and started to get up.

"We better go see what's wrong."

I grabbed his arm and yanked him back down on the bed.

"I'll go. You always get caught."

I got out of bed as quietly as I could and went to the door. At the hall, I got down on my belly, like a soldier in the army. I didn't make a sound. I didn't even breathe deeply as I crawled to where the hall went into the living room. I peeked around the corner.

The tree was there, just as we left it last night, with all the decorations and bulbs and lights. Then . . . my head jerked back and my eyes popped wide open.

There weren't any presents under the tree!

I looked all around the room. Mama and Daddy weren't there either. There wasn't any video camera. No lights. And *no* Mama and Daddy.

Still crawling on my stomach, I backed up to the bedroom doorway. I got to my knees and motioned to Jimmy.

"You better come look."

He frowned, then trotted over to where I was and got down on his knees.

Jimmy crawled to the living room on his stomach. I came up beside him on my hands and knees. My head was only a couple of inches above his as we both peeked around the corner at the same time. Jimmy jerked—kind of like I did when I saw there weren't any presents. The top of his head clunked me on the chin. My teeth clanked together and stars popped out in front of my eyes.

"Ouch," I said, grabbing my chin. I scrambled to my feet and thought about kicking him. I didn't though, since I figured he hadn't meant to hit me that hard.

Jimmy got to his feet, too. He leaned around the corner, looking long and hard at the empty spot under the tree before turning to me.

"What's the deal?"

I shrugged. Then, feeling like maybe it was a trick or something, I grabbed his arm and pulled him back around the corner.

"Mama? Daddy?" I called. "Can we come out now?"

There was no answer.

Jimmy winked at me when he figured out what I was up to.

"Yeah," he added. "We're tired of sittin' on the bed. Can we get up?"

Still there was no answer.

Boldly, we both stepped into the living room. I marched over to the kitchen and looked behind the bar. Jimmy looked under the couch.

"Get up from there," I scoffed. "They wouldn't hide under the couch."

Jimmy joined me in the kitchen. Daddy's coffee was gurgling and bubbling in the coffeepot, but there was no sign of either of them. The back door was open, so I started for it. Jimmy came with me.

I couldn't see anything through the storm door, so I opened it and peeked outside. Daddy was standing at the corner of the house in his sweats with the video camera on his shoulder.

The second he saw my eyeball peeking through the crack, he started shooting. I could tell because I could hear the camera clicking. Mama was in her robe, right at the corner of the house. She waited until Jimmy and I stepped out on the porch before snapping a picture and disappearing around the edge of the house.

"Something weird is going on," I told Jimmy.

He grunted his agreement.

Daddy kept shooting film with his video as Mama's arm appeared and waved for us to come. We were only about halfway to where Daddy was when he stopped shooting and vanished around the side of the house where Mama had gone.

As careful as a pair of cats sneaking up on a bird, Jimmy and I crept along toward the corner. We made a wide arc, away from the brick wall, and when we were where we could see our side yard, there was Mama flashing pictures as fast as she could, and Daddy shooting video film. He was smiling so hard you could see his grin on either side of the camera, and . . .

and standing between them was the most beautiful horse I had ever seen.

It was a pinto—mostly white with some big, brown spots.

"Look what Santa left," Daddy called.

"Well?" Mama stopped shooting pictures. "What do you think of him?"

Jimmy and I stood with our mouths gaping open.

It was the best Christmas present, ever!

CHAPTER
9

Jimmy got to ride first. That's because he'd been sick. Mama and Daddy must have figured we'd be so excited that it would be hard to make us go back inside and get our warm clothes.

They let us look at the horse for a moment, then Mama reached down beside her camera case and tossed Jimmy and me our jackets. Inside them, she had wrapped our socks and shoes.

As soon as we had our stuff on, Daddy grabbed Jimmy and set him up on the saddle. Then he led the horse around the yard.

I remember shivering so hard that I couldn't stop. I wasn't cold though. Just excited. I couldn't seem to hold still.

Mama went inside and got my heavy coat anyway. Then it was my turn.

I wanted to ride the horse myself. Daddy wouldn't let me. He said the horse needed to get used to us and we needed to get used to him, and for right now, he'd lead him around.

After a while, he made me get off and put Jimmy back on. Then I got to go again and Daddy gave me the reins.

"Don't run him. Just walk around the yard." He looked down at his watch. "I'll time you, then we'll let Jimmy have a turn."

Jimmy and I kept taking turns until all four of us were blue from the cold.

I had been trembling from being so excited. Now my teeth were rattling together and my feet hurt. Even so, when Mama said it was time for Daddy to take the saddle off and for us to go in, I didn't want to.

Jimmy and I both jumped up and down and begged and pleaded to ride just one more time. Finally, Daddy stomped his foot. He pointed a big finger at the back door.

"Inside. NOW!!!"

It took a little while to get warmed up. Jimmy and I went to our rooms and put on our fuzzy slippers and our sweat pants. Then we came back and drank some hot cocoa that Mama had fixed with marshmallows on the top. It was good.

Daddy drank his coffee and kept telling Jimmy and me to come and sit down, because we kept running to the door to look out at our horse every ten seconds or so.

When we finally quit shivering, Mama went into the garage and came back with some packages wrapped in shiny paper with bright bows. Poky, our beagle, followed her into the house. Mama and Daddy had put him in the garage because they didn't know if he'd bark at the new horse.

Mama's nose kind of crinkled up when she spotted Poky. With her foot, she shoved him back into the garage.

"Soon as it warms up, you boys need to give that dog a bath. He *stinks*!"

Then she held out the packages.

"Santa must have left these in the garage so you wouldn't trip over them when you were running to look at your horse," she said with a twinkle in her eye.

We followed her to the living room. When she put the packages down near the tree, Jimmy and I started ripping paper and throwing bows and giggling and downright tearing into stuff.

Jimmy got socks and pants and shirts and sweaters and a real cowboy hat and a double-holster set of six-shooters with pearl handles. (They were really plastic, I think, but they looked like pearl handles.) Pretty as the six-shooters were, his favorite present was the hat. Daddy showed him inside where it said STETSON.

"That's not a toy or a little kid's hat," he told Jimmy. "It's a real, honest-to-goodness Stetson. Just like the cowboys used to wear."

Jimmy set it on his head. It was just the right size and didn't even smush his ears down.

He was kind of a funny sight when he strapped his six-shooters on over his sweats and stuck on his hat and went galloping around the house pretending he was on a roundup.

I got a bunch of shirts and sweaters and a new pair of tennis shoes. I also got some games for our video. I knew I'd have to share them with Jimmy, but I didn't mind. In the last package I opened there were a pair of spurs and a repeater rifle and a six-shooter with wooden handles—well, they were plastic, but they looked as good as real wood. The spurs weren't real either. They were made out of tin or something with a little star that spun around at the back. They all came in a set that said YOUNG GUNS REAL LIFE OUTFITTERS.

The rifle was my favorite thing. It had a lever and made a popping sound when I cocked and shot it.

Mama said we could play cowboys, but we either had to stay in the house or in the front yard because all the shooting might scare our new horse.

We played in the house, then got dressed in our warm clothes and played outside.

After lunch, Daddy let us ride again. We named our horse Buck. He didn't buck, but it seemed like a good name for a cowboy horse. When we went in, Jimmy wanted to play with our toy guns, but I wanted to play with my new video games. Jimmy asked if he could borrow my spurs so he could play cowboy by himself.

I plugged the video game into the machine and frowned at him. Then when I saw the way his eyebrows arched up real high and how his face looked so excited, I figured: Well, he's been sick and he *is* my brother . . .

"Okay," I answered. "But you be careful with them. Don't go messin' 'em up."

He took off like a shot.

I played all three of my new video games. The Surfer USA wasn't much fun. I kept falling off the board and drowning. Contra was okay. It was kind of an army game where you shot at the enemy. My favorite was Spy Chase. With that one, I got to shoot cars with my machine gun and bump them off the road. You had to watch out for the big blue car that snuck up behind you though. You couldn't shoot it, and it'd knock you off the road if you weren't careful.

It wasn't dark yet, but it was starting to cool off. I heard Mama call Jimmy to come into the house, but he didn't want to. That didn't surprise me.

What did surprise me was he didn't come in and try to take over the video game. He went to his room instead.

I figured he was going to put away his cowboy stuff. As soon as he'd finished, he'd show up and want to play.

After a while, when he hadn't shown up, I got to wondering about him and went to see what was going on.

When I got to his room, Jimmy's door was shut. I tapped on it. There was no answer, so I peeked in.

Jimmy was lying across his bed. He was on his tummy and I could see his sides kind of pouching in and out like he was crying.

I slipped in the door and shut it behind me.

"What's wrong?"

Jimmy looked up at me. His eyes were red. "I'm sorry," he moaned, and that was all.

I tilted my head to the side.

"Sorry about what?"

He let out a loud "Boohoo" and tried to cover his face with the pillow.

I sat on the edge of the bed and patted his back.

"What's wrong, Jimmy? What are you sorry about? Are you feeling sick again?"

He buried his head farther into the pillow.

I rubbed his back.

"Come on, Jimmy. I'm your brother. You can tell me. You mad at Mama for making you come in? You upset because . . ."

There was something in his hand. Without raising his face from the pillow, he brought his hand behind his back and put it where I was rubbing.

"I broke 'em," I could hear him say between muffled sobs. "I didn't mean to. The star fell off."

I took the things he handed me. They were the spurs that had come with the six-shooter and the Young Guns rifle. One of the stars was missing and the back part of the spur was bent.

I looked at the spurs, then glared at the back of my brother's head.

Jimmy was always getting into my stuff. Ever since he

was old enough to walk, he'd tear up my things or get toys out of my toy box and get me in trouble for not picking up the mess. I wanted to bop him on the seat, hard as I could.

Then . . . I looked down at him. I couldn't believe how little he looked. His sides heaved in and out with his crying.

I swatted him playfully on the bottom.

"Quit your bawling. It's no big deal. They were just little play-toy things anyway."

He rolled over and looked at me. The tears streamed down his cheeks.

"I didn't mean to," he whined. "I'm always messing up your stuff. I . . ."

"Oh, come on." I shook his leg and laughed. "I'll help you look for it."

We went outside to Poky's doghouse. Jimmy climbed on top of it and started kicking it with his heels, pretending it was a bucking bronco.

"This is where I was." He wiped his nose on his sleeve. "It was the right one." He pointed. "The one over here is what fell off."

I got down on my hands and knees. Poky came up and tried to lick me in the face. I shoved him back, because he hadn't had a bath yet, and he still stunk.

There were little marks along the side of the doghouse where some of the paint had chipped off. But no star. Jimmy got down with me. We looked all over the place, dug around in the grass, lifted the doghouse up on its side, even looked around the sidewalk, figuring maybe it flew over there.

No star from my spur.

At first I was kind of mad about it, but when I started pretending—for Jimmy's sake—that I didn't care, I found out that I really didn't.

He took it hard though. He kept saying how sorry he was and kept sniffling. I ruffled his hair and made him come and play the video games with me.

After a while, he quit worrying about it.

That night though, after the lights were out and we were in our beds, Jimmy snuck into my room.

I was kind of in that dreamy world, right before you doze off. He plopped something down on my stomach. I jumped. It was dark in my room, so I started feeling around to see what Jimmy had put on me.

"I want you to have my real cowboy Stetson hat." He made a gulping sound. "It'll pay you back for me losing the star out of your spurs."

I finally found the hat that he'd put on my stomach. I sat up.

"I don't want your hat," I mumbled, still half asleep.

"I want you to have it," Jimmy said.

I yawned. Then I scooted up in bed and flipped on the light so I could look Jimmy straight in the eye.

"Look," I said in my sternest whisper, "Daddy got you a really good hat. It's yours. I didn't even like those dumb spurs. Now, take your hat and go back to your room so I can get some sleep."

"But . . . but . . ." he stammered.

I grabbed his arm and pulled him across me.

"Jimmy. I mean it. It's dumb to try to trade a real hat for fake spurs. Besides, I'm tired of you worrying about it. If you don't take your hat and go to bed, I'm . . . I'm . . ." I reached down and started tickling his ribs. "I'm gonna tickle you to death."

He started giggling and squealing and squirming around. That high-pitched laugh made the chills pop up on the back of my neck.

"What's going on down there?" I heard Mama call from her room.

I let go of Jimmy. He slapped a hand over his mouth, trying to quit laughing.

"Nothing," I called back. "Jimmy and I were just . . . ah . . . visiting."

"It's time for bed," Daddy's gruff voice called. "You two can visit in the morning."

Jimmy got up and stood beside the bed.

"Are you sure you don't want it?"

I picked up the hat and stuck it on his head.

"I'm sure."

He leaned over and kissed me on the cheek. It was one of those wet, sloppy kisses. Only, I didn't wipe it off until Jimmy was back in his room and the light was out.

CHAPTER
10

I was glad I made Jimmy keep his hat, because by April, all his hair fell out.

I guess it was a month before that, in March or so, when his leukemia started acting up again. He and Mama had to start going back to the doctor's for treatments. They went on the first and third Sunday of each month. But just like when Jimmy first started his treatments, he didn't get to come home as soon as they expected and ended up staying two or three days each time.

Jimmy always hated to go. He wouldn't cry in front of Mama and Daddy though, because that made *them* cry.

He told me so.

Sometimes at night when we were in our rooms, he would sneak across the hall and lie down in bed with me. We'd talk about things. He'd tell me how he didn't like getting stuck with needles and how he didn't like having to sleep away from home—but he knew he had to because it was the only way he could get well.

Jimmy was scared. I was, too, but I tried not to let on.

Anyway, by April, every bit of his hair was gone. He didn't want anyone to see him with his head bald and shiny, so he kept his Stetson on almost all the time. I even went into his room one night to see how he was and he had it on in bed.

Mama and Daddy and the doctors promised him it would grow back. But by Easter, when I got out of school for Easter break, he was still bald and shiny.

We took Mama and Jimmy to the hospital on Sunday. Daddy stayed home on Monday and in the morning we went down to help work on the church building. Around noon, Mama called and said the medicine didn't make Jimmy sick this time, so Daddy and I jumped in the car to go get them. After we picked them up, Mama explained that the doctors told her that Jimmy wouldn't have to come back—at least for a while. Mama and Daddy took us to a nice restaurant. Everything was so good, we almost made ourselves sick.

We were too full for dessert, but Mama and Daddy asked for another cup of coffee. While they were waiting for the waitress to bring it, Daddy snuck off to use the phone. I figured he was calling some more people about the speakers for the church. Only, when he came back, he was real bouncy. There was a great big smile on his face.

"I had this planned for tomorrow or Wednesday," he

said, "but since we got finished early at the doctor's, and since we don't have to go back for a while . . . well . . ."

Nobody knew what he was talking about and when we asked, he wouldn't tell us. He just smiled and shifted in his chair.

In fact, Daddy was so wiggly, we left the restaurant before he even finished the coffee he asked for. We drove across town. We parked in the lot next to the Cowboy Hall of Fame.

The Cowboy Hall of Fame is one of the neatest things in all of Oklahoma. It's not as neat as the Wichita Mountains or the Illinois River or the Arbuckle Mountains, but God made those things. People built the Cowboy Hall of Fame. They did a pretty good job—for people.

It was a great big building with a whole bunch of flags in front. There were arches and a fountain that bubbled and shot water way up in the air.

I had been to see it once before, when I was in second grade. The neat stuff was in the basement. That's where the scenes of honest-to-goodness cowboys and cattle drives and saloons with a player piano that still worked and things like that were. It was "real live" junk instead of just pictures or statues. There was a room with photos of cowboy movie stars and a special room with John Wayne stuff in it.

I remember that when I went on the school field trip, I didn't get to see as much of the exhibits as I wanted to. We had to hurry so we could eat dinner and get the buses back to school. Besides, Miss Parks, my second-grade teacher, had to keep yelling at Beth Simms and Randy Yorkton to keep their fingers off the statues and to get down off the chuck wagon—since they weren't even supposed to be back there. Anyway, I was looking forward to seeing the place with Mama and Daddy, because I knew they'd let Jimmy and me spend as much time as we wanted looking at the interesting stuff. They'd even let us explore on our own.

We didn't get to explore on our own.

Daddy left us sitting on some benches beneath the flags. They fluttered and popped in the Oklahoma wind. Beside us, we could see the fountains shooting water into the air and hear them gurgling.

Daddy was inside for a long, long time. When he came out, there was a man with him. He was a big man, tall with wide shoulders. He had a fat tummy that hung over a big, silver belt buckle.

He had a happy face though. There were wrinkles around his eyes and the corners of his mouth that made his smile look easy and natural. He tugged at the brim of the rumpled cowboy hat that sat kind of cockeyed on his head.

"Mrs. Tipton," he grinned at Mama, "my name is Gerald Scott. I'm the director here at the hall. Your husband tells me you have a couple of young gentlemen who are interested in cowboys."

Mama's mouth kind of flopped open. It made a "clunk" sound when she closed it. She glanced at us, then nodded.

"I thought y'all might like a private tour," Mr. Scott went

on. "You know, maybe look around a little and see what goes on behind the scenes. We might even open a few of the display cases and let the boys have a close-up look at some of our more special items."

My eyes popped out so much, I thought they were going to fall out of my head. Mama's mouth had flopped open again. But when she turned and saw the look on our faces, she smiled.

"I think the boys would like that, Mr. Scott."

When we followed Mr. Scott inside, a young man walked up and shook hands with him, then with Daddy.

He was kind of short, but he was so skinny, it almost made him look tall. He had on a rumpled-up cowboy hat and boots. His white shirt looked stiff as a board, because it was so crisp and clean. He had on blue jeans.

"My name's Les Benton." He smiled, turning to shake Jimmy's hand. "Your dad and I visited on the phone. He's told me a lot about you and . . ."

I never heard the rest of what he told Jimmy because when he said his name, I got so excited, I started dancing from foot to foot.

Les Benton was just about the most famous Oklahoman since Will Rogers or three-time All-Around Champion Rodeo Cowboy, Jim Shoulders. I mean . . . Les Benton had been *World Champion Cowboy* for the last two years straight! He could ride buckin' broncs, rope calves, ride bulls . . . He was the greatest real live cowboy in the whole wide world!!!

*   *   *

It was some day.

Les Benton and Mr. Scott showed us *everything* in the Cowboy Hall of Fame. Mr. Scott had a pocketful of keys. Every time he or Les saw that Jimmy or I really seemed interested in something, he'd get his keys out and open up the case for us. We got to hold Les Benton's trophy belt buckles. We got to rattle his spurs. We got to hold Jim Shoulders's trophy. It was so big, it took both Jimmy and me to hold it up while Daddy took our picture.

Jimmy tried on Jim Shoulders's boots, too. They came up to his knees, and he looked kind of silly in them. He started giggling when he tried to walk. That high, shrill laugh of his started all of us chuckling.

Down in the basement, Mr. Scott climbed up on a ladder to reach a lock at the top of the case with John Wayne's six-shooter and rifle. He opened the case and handed the pistol to Jimmy and the rifle to me. He told us that these were the actual guns that John Wayne used in his movies. He told us how many movies, but I couldn't remember.

Mr. Scott disappeared through a door. It went somewhere behind the cases. In a minute, he came back with two cowboy hats.

"These belonged to John Wayne, too," he said. "This one," he added, handing one of the hats to me, "was the one he wore in the movie, *The Shootist*. And this one," he said, giving the other to Jimmy, "this one he wore in *True Grit* and *The Cowboys*."

I put mine on. It fell down over my ears and I couldn't even see out.

Jimmy didn't want to take his cowboy hat off. He stood there, kind of shifting from one foot to the other and looking at the hat in his hand.

Mr. Scott smiled. "Don't you want to try it?"

Jimmy didn't answer.

"Your dad told me that *The Cowboys* is your favorite movie. That's the hat John Wayne wore when they were filming."

Jimmy's bottom lip stuck out. It quivered. Mr. Scott got down on one knee in front of Jimmy. He looked around, like he was making sure nobody else was watching. Then he took off his hat and rubbed his head.

Mr. Scott was just as bald and shiny as Jimmy. In fact, his head almost seemed to glow. Smiling, he looked Jimmy square in the eye, winked, then put his hat back on. Jimmy handed Daddy his Stetson and put on John Wayne's hat.

It was the neatest day I've ever had. Mr. Scott took us everyplace. We saw everything there was to see in the Cowboy Hall of Fame.

Before we left, Les Benton went upstairs. We followed with Mr. Scott. Les was waiting outside with his champion roping horse. He said the horse had too much "spirit" for us to ride by ourselves, but he lifted Jimmy up in the saddle and they rode all over the whole, entire grounds at the Cowboy Hall of Fame. Then I got to ride. We galloped, we trotted, we ran, we dodged around trees and statues. We even jumped the little stream that flowed into the big pool where the fountains were.

It was the greatest day—ever!

I figured Jimmy would be tired and sleepy on the drive home. We had had a pretty busy day. Instead of falling asleep, he kept taking his hat off and putting it back on. He would frown at it, kind of wiggle the brim, turn it around and around, then stick it back on.

I didn't think too much about it—not until that night.

CHAPTER

11

The bed sure felt good. I guess being excited and doing neat stuff wears you out almost as much as hard work. I flipped over and turned out my light. It was still kind of early, but I didn't care. I needed a good night's sleep.

I fluffed my pillow, but before I closed my eyes, I decided to see if Jimmy was asleep yet. I lifted my head and peeked over my big toes.

His light was out, but he wasn't asleep. I could see him. He sat on the edge of his bed. He had his hat in his hand. The glow from his night-light shone on his bald head.

I told him to quit messin' with his hat and go to sleep. He did.

The next morning, Jimmy got up before I did. I guess it was the noise from the TV that woke me. I yawned and sat up. Then I staggered into the living room to see why he was up so early.

Jimmy was watching *The Cowboys* on the VCR. I yawned again and sat down to watch with him. Only, he punched the fast-forward button. Then he punched it again. Then he got the *True Grit* tape out and fast-forwarded his way through it. Finally, he got out *Rio Lobo* and did the same with that tape.

"Who can watch a movie with you punching that fast-forward button all the time?" I griped. "Either let me watch the show or turn it off."

Jimmy didn't fuss back. When I griped at him, he almost always griped back. He didn't say a word. I looked over at him.

He was holding his hat again, frowning at it. I noticed a little tear leak from the corner of his left eye.

I tilted my head to the side.

"What's wrong, Jimmy?"

He looked up at me and sniffed. "My hat's not any good."

My eyes scrunched up. "What do you mean, it's not any good? It's a Stetson. It's one of the best."

Jimmy just shook his head.

"It's not a *real* cowboy hat." He frowned.

I got up and went to sit beside him on the couch. "What do you mean—'not real'?"

"I mean, it's clean and pretty and . . ." He wiped his nose with the sleeve of his pajamas. ". . . and it just doesn't look like the ones we saw at the Cowboy Hall of Fame. It's not like John Wayne's or Les Benton's." Then, with a nod of his head, he motioned at the TV. "And it's not like the ones the real cowboys in the movies wear either."

I pulled my heels up right next to my bottom on the cushion and rested my chin on my knees. I sat for a long time watching the TV and wondering what in the world Jimmy was talking about.

Finally it sunk in, like the shock from a finger stuck in a light socket. I jerked.

"Oh, you mean the way they look kind of dirty and bent up?"

Jimmy smiled and nodded.

I shook my head. "That's 'cause their hats are old. Yours is still kind of new. If you wear it long enough, your hat will look like theirs, too."

Jimmy jabbed a finger at the screen. "What's that line around the hatband?"

John Wayne took his hat off and wiped the inside of the brim with his red bandanna.

"It's a sweat line," I told Jimmy. "It's a stain from wearing the hat and sweating in it. Cowboys wear their hats when they chase cows or fight bad guys or build fences. All sorts of stuff that gets them hot and sweaty. They wear them when they're riding horses and it's hot and dusty. They wear them in the rain. After a while," I said with a shrug, "they just get to looking like that. Yours will, too—after a while."

Jimmy looked at his hat. He shook his head and looked over at me.

"I don't want it to look like a real cowboy hat—after a while. I want it to look like a real cowboy hat—now!"

I noticed another tear leak from his eye.

"I'm gonna go throw it in the dirt and jump up and down on it, some. I'm gonna put it in Poky's water pan, and then put dirt on it."

"You can't do that. If you stomp on it or get it wet, all the shape will go out of it. You still want it to have the shape of a cowboy hat, don't you?"

"Yeah."

With a jerk of my head, I motioned toward our bedrooms. "Come on. Let's get dressed and I'll help you with your hat. Between us, we'll get it looking like a real, honest-to-goodness cowboy hat."

CHAPTER

12

Jimmy and I did just about everything to that poor hat. We went out and rode Buck. Jimmy let the hat fall off and land on the ground a couple of times. We chased Poky all over the backyard, caught him, and gave him a bath. Jimmy wore the hat and leaned down real close to Poky when he shook to dry himself off. We even played Frisbee with it. Jimmy would stand on one side of the yard, I'd stand on the other, and we'd sail the hat back and forth.

Jimmy had put newspaper inside the hat because when his hair fell out, the hat was too big for him. Every day after school, when I would come home he would take the paper out and stick the hat on my head. Then, we'd go out in the yard and he'd throw passes to me with the football. I'd run and run and run, until I got sweated up. Then, I'd smush the hat down on my head and run some more. Jimmy even talked me into running laps around the block a couple of times. After a few weeks, with all the sweating I did, Jimmy and I finally noticed a small, dark stain starting to form—above the hatband.

Mostly, though, we just managed to get it dirty. That—and it started to smell a little, too. Mama noticed it one morning in church.

None of the men at the First Christian Church ever wore hats. And when or if they did, they took them off before they came into the sanctuary.

Jimmy always wore his.

Nobody ever said anything about it. Reverend Parks told him it was okay. Our church was small and everybody knew that Jimmy had lost his hair—so nobody told him to take the hat off or looked at him funnylike.

The first Sunday in May, I sat with my family, instead of in the balcony as I usually did. We were singing "Holy, Holy, Holy" when I heard Mama sniffing. I looked up at her. She'd quit singing and had sort of a strange frown on her face. She sniffed again and again—each time, her nose brought her closer and closer to Jimmy's hat. Between verse two and verse three, I heard her whisper to him:

"Soon as we get home, that hat's getting a good cleaning."

Jimmy's bottom lip pouched out. He reached up with both hands and pulled the hat down over his ears.

*   *   *

The real action started when we got home. Mama found a little brush. She asked Jimmy to give the hat to her. Jimmy must have forgotten what she'd said in church, because when she asked for the hat and he looked up and saw the brush—he acted startled.

Jimmy yanked the hat down over his ears. Mama talked to him nicely and tried to reason with him. But it didn't work. When she tried to lift the hat off, he clung to the brim like a bulldog chomping down on a bone.

"Jimmy," she scolded, "that hat is filthy. It stinks! You give it to me right now!"

"No!" Jimmy squealed and took off for his room.

Mama was hot on his heels.

I raced after them to Jimmy's bedroom. Mama almost got hold of him, but he dove across his bed. She walked around, only he crawled under. Mama circled again and just as she reached for him, Jimmy dove across the bed once more. This time, Mama dove after him.

It looked kind of funny—Mama in her church dress, diving across Jimmy's bed. Her feet with the high-heeled shoes kicked in the air as she crawled and clambered over the mattress. Jimmy hit the floor on the other side and rolled under the bed. Mama grabbed hold of his foot. Half off the bed, she struggled to catch Jimmy, her Sunday dress and white slip fluttering like a flag.

She managed to get hold of his shoe, but it slipped off in her hand.

When it did, Jimmy crawled underneath the bed and

shot out on the other side. Still clinging to his hat, he tore off down the hall toward the living room.

Mama finally managed to get to her feet and smooth her dress down. As she wheeled around and started after him, I jumped in front of her.

I was going to explain about Jimmy's hat. I was going to tell her why we were getting it dirty. But, when I looked at Mama's eyes, I forgot what I was going to say. Her eyes looked like melted pools of lava from a volcano. They were deep and big around, and hot! Her jaw stuck out. Her teeth were clamped together like the steel vise Daddy used down at the church when he was putting the corner braces together.

My breath made a whistling sound as I sucked it in.

"It's Jimmy's hat," was all I could manage.

Mama glared at me.

"It stinks!" she snarled at me. "Now shut up and MOVE!"

She roared the word "move" instead of saying it. I got out of her way.

Jimmy was determined to hang onto his hat. Mama was determined to clean it. I figured the smartest thing for me to do was just stay out of it. So I went to the living room and found a book. Mama chased Jimmy all over the house, then all over the backyard, then all over the house again before she finally got the hat.

I'd never seen my mama act like that. How things got so out of hand—I don't know! It all started off innocently enough—but someplace along the line, it turned into a real battle. I kept out of it. I just sat, acting like I was reading the book, and listened to the whole thing. I pretended I wasn't listening though.

Daddy missed out on it.

This was his Sunday to drive the church van. Our church has a blue-colored van that picks up the old people who are in wheelchairs or who don't have a ride to church. After church the driver takes them home again.

By the time Daddy got in, all the action was over. Mama was in the kitchen. She had the steam iron set on end so the steam would poof up while she scrubbed the hat. Jimmy was in his room, bawling. I was still sitting quiet as a mouse, reading my book.

Daddy was happy to be home. He trotted into the kitchen. "Hi, honey." He smiled happily. "What's for dinner?"

It was the wrong thing to say.

Mama glanced up and snarled at him. The steam from the iron helped her clean Jimmy's hat. It also made her bangs droop down over her forehead. Even from the living room, I could see her glaring eyes, shining from underneath her droopy bangs.

When Daddy saw the look, he took a step back.

"Is something wrong?"

Mama didn't say anything. She just went back to brushing the dirt off Jimmy's hat.

Daddy came to me. "What's going on?" he asked.

I shrugged.

Then he went to Jimmy's room. Jimmy didn't answer. He just bawled and boohooed from where he was curled up under his bed.

Scratching his head, Daddy came back to the living room. There was a sort of dumb, confused look on his face. He stood there, looking toward Mama. She brushed the hat with a vengeance—as if she were trying to scrub the felt clear off it. Then Daddy looked back toward Jimmy's room. We could hear my brother whimpering.

I could tell by the look on Daddy's face that he was trying to sort stuff out. He knew something bad was going on—only nobody would talk to him!

He kept scratching his head and looking back and forth. I could almost see the wheels spinning inside his brain. I could almost hear him thinking—Mama's mad. Jimmy's crying. Then, looking at me, his eyes narrowed. And Nick's trying to look real innocent and pretending to read a book.

He snapped his fingers and pointed at the door.

"Backyard. NOW!"

Once we were alone outside, I explained the whole thing. I told him about how Jimmy wanted his hat to look like the *real* cowboy hats he'd seen at the Cowboy Hall of Fame. I told him how Mama got to smelling it in church and how it really *did* stink—kind of. And I told him about the big fight.

"I didn't know Mama had such a temper," I confided in him.

Daddy smiled.

"She *does* have a temper, but she usually keeps it under control—at least with you and Jimmy. Things just got a little out of hand. Once she understands how Jimmy feels, she'll be okay." He glanced toward the house. I saw his tongue make a circle inside his mouth. It pushed his lips and cheeks out as he moved it around. "But right now isn't the time to discuss it."

Daddy nudged my shoulder with an elbow. "Come on. I know how to fix Jimmy's hat. We'll go get lunch and let your mother cool off a bit."

Jimmy was still curled up under his bed. He wouldn't come out, not even for Daddy. Daddy didn't argue with him. He just reached under the bed and pulled Jimmy out by one leg.

With Jimmy tucked under his arm like a limp football, he marched through the living room to the front door. "The boys and I are going after Kentucky Fried Chicken," he called to Mama. "We'll be back in a few minutes."

While we waited in line at the drive-through window, Daddy told Jimmy and me that we were going about this hat deal all wrong.

"Cowboys don't wear dirty hats," he explained. "Their hats look like they do because they're weathered."

"What's weathered?" Jimmy wondered out loud.

"Well," Daddy said, clearing his throat, "you don't want it looking all stiff and clean, right?"

Jimmy nodded.

"But you don't want it looking or smelling so bad that nobody wants to get close to you. Right?"

Jimmy shrugged.

"You just want it to look . . . well . . . natural. Right?"

Jimmy smiled. Daddy smiled back and patted Jimmy's bald head. Jimmy rubbed where Daddy had patted. "But what's weathered?"

Daddy put the car in gear and scooted us up. We were next in line now.

"I'll show you when we get home," he said. "It's easier to show you than to explain. When I tell your mom what's going on—I bet she'll even help us with it."

Jimmy nibbled at his bottom lip.

"You reckon she's still gonna be mad at me?"

"No." Daddy laughed and pulled up to the window. "By the time we get her fed, she'll have forgotten all about it."

CHAPTER
13

"I made a complete idiot out of myself," Mama told Jimmy.

This was after we finished lunch and after she and Daddy disappeared into the kitchen to do the dishes (which I thought was sort of funny because we didn't get any dishes dirty since we brought everything from the Kentucky Fried Chicken place).

Mama was down on one knee in front of Jimmy. He scooted up to the edge of the couch. He wrapped his arms around her and they hugged for a long, long time.

Finally, Mama got to her feet. She helped Jimmy up and motioned for me. "We're all going to help Jimmy make his hat look like a real cowboy hat. Nick, your dad needs your help out in the garage. Jimmy, we have to find something in my closet. Will you help me while Nick's helping Daddy?"

Jimmy nodded with one of his great big smiles.

In the garage, Daddy was digging around in his storage bin for something. When he saw me, he told me to get his saw and cut a ten-inch piece off a big two-by-twelve-inch board in the corner. My arm got a little tired before I had it cut, but Daddy found what he was looking for and came to help me finish.

We went back to the kitchen and met Mama and Jimmy. Mama was carrying a Styrofoam "head." It was sort of like one of those heads on the dummies you see in the stores. Only this one was made out of white Styrofoam and didn't have eyes. It was shaped like a head though—with a nose and lips and dents where the eyes were supposed to be.

I remembered seeing it before. It was when I was little— a long time ago. It was right before Christmas and I had been prowling around in Mama's closet to see if I could find any presents stashed there. When I had first seen it, there was a funny-looking pile of blond hair on top of the head. I had asked Mama about it. She'd told me it was a "wig holder" for a wig she used to wear when she was in college. She also told me not to be messing around in her closet!

I couldn't help wondering what had happened to the hair . . . I mean, wig.

Daddy had Mama hold the head while he wrapped a bunch of heavy gray duct tape around the bottom of it. Then he told me to put the board I had cut on the table. He took some shingle nails—the ones with the big heads that carpenters use to put shingles on houses—and drove them through the taped part of the head and into the board.

"The big board will keep the head from blowing over if the wind gets up," he said. "And the tape will keep the nails from tearing up the Styrofoam."

We took the head outside. There, Daddy got Jimmy's hat and put it on top of the head. Mama handed him some long pins she brought from her room. Daddy stuck four pins through the hat and into the head. Then he got the stepladder out of the garage. There was a little place on the chimney where it went from the wide base to the narrow smokestack. The roof hung over the little sunk-in place. He gave the hat to Jimmy, to make sure he was tall enough to reach the ledge from the top of the ladder.

"Your hat needs to be out in the weather a little bit," Daddy said as Jimmy put the hat-holder contraption we had built on the ledge. "But if you leave it out in the rain and snow—it'll get too much weather. Then, it'll start to droop and lose its shape. Putting it under the edge of the house will let it get the morning dew. That way it'll get a little moisture on it, but it won't get *too* wet."

He pointed a finger at the back fence. "It will catch a little of the early morning sun coming over the fence. So, each night when you put it up, you need to give it a quarter-turn. That way it will fade evenly, instead of just on one side." Daddy steadied the ladder while Jimmy started down. "It's gonna take awhile, son, but before long, it's gonna start looking like a real cowboy hat. Nice and soft and natural. That . . ." He smiled at Mama. "That . . . and it won't smell from you and Nick sweating it all up and throwing it around in the horse lot. Okay?"

Jimmy's chest puffed out big.

"Okay!"

Putting his hat on the little ledge beneath the eave of the house became almost a religion to Jimmy. Every night, right before he went to sleep, he'd put the hat on the head and pin it down. Then he'd slip his shoes on and climb the ladder to put it up by the chimney.

Every morning he took it down and stuck it on his head.

Within a month, it started looking like what Daddy called "natural."

I've never seen a little kid SO proud of anything! Every time Jimmy put it on, his chest would puff up and his smile would stretch clean across his face. Jimmy *loved* his real, honest-to-goodness cowboy hat!

In late May, we found out that on Sunday afternoons, Jimmy was going to have to go back to the doctor's for more treatments. I didn't want him and Mama to go back. I spent all Saturday night tossing and turning and worrying about them.

At Sunday school the next morning, Mrs. Barker asked us to think of all the miracles we could remember from our Bible lessons. She told us to think about our favorites.

I couldn't think of any.

When she asked us to talk about them, Jack Fitch said he liked the one where Moses made that big ocean part so the people who were running away from the Egyptians could get across. Bethany Sparks said her favorite was when

Moses made his stick turn into a snake and when he made
the grasshoppers eat up the Egyptians. Mrs. Barker told
her that grasshoppers didn't eat the Egyptians, but they ate
up the crops instead.

Kyle Clements said his favorite was when Jesus and this
bunch of guys were out in a boat and a storm came up and
he told the storm to shut up and it did. Mrs. Barker said
that she doubted Jesus told the storm to "shut up," but she
thought he was pretty close to the story anyhow. Bart
Drummond thought the big flood that came and the huge
boat that Moses built was neat. Mrs. Barker said it was
Noah, not Moses.

When she asked me, all I could do was sit and stare at
her. I couldn't think about anything but Jimmy having to go
back to those dumb old doctors.

I didn't answer, and Mrs. Barker didn't make me. She
talked to the others about miracles and how nowadays lots
of people didn't believe in miracles anymore. She told us
that we all thought of big, exciting miracles. Then she said
that there were little miracles, too. Miracles didn't always
have to be big and dramatic and exciting and then . . .

Then . . . I didn't listen anymore, because I couldn't
keep from thinking about my little brother.

While I sat alone in the balcony during church, I decided
the best miracle I could think of would be if Jimmy didn't
have to go to the doctor's anymore.

That afternoon, though, we took him anyway.

*   *   *

It was three days before Jimmy and Mama got to come home. Jimmy looked pale and he seemed weak and tired. He even asked me if I would go put his hat on the white Styrofoam head under the eave of the house.

That night, I heard him flopping around in his bedroom. "Be still and go to sleep," I called.

"Nick?" he called back.

"What is it?"

His voice was real soft, so Mama and Daddy couldn't hear him.

"If I die, I want you to have my hat."

I almost choked on the knot in my throat. I spent the whole night flouncing around on my bed. I wrapped the pillow over my head. I kicked the covers off. I pulled the covers back over me. I twisted and turned and flipped and flopped—all night long. I don't think I got a wink of sleep.

I never heard another peep out of my brother. Jimmy slept just fine.

CHAPTER
14

Jimmy slept a lot.

It got to where by the middle of June he hardly ever played with me. He didn't feel like riding Buck. Buck was about the greatest horse that ever was, but without Jimmy to ride with me, I didn't much want to ride either.

It was also in June that we started going to Reverend Parks for what Mama and Daddy called "counseling." I didn't know what counseling was. At school, we had a counselor. She was the person you got sent to if you got in trouble in class. She didn't spank anybody or make them stay after school. She just talked about getting in trouble.

I guess we went to counseling because we were in trouble and needed to talk. It was a different kind of trouble from what you get into at school—but trouble, nonetheless.

Sometimes Reverend Parks talked to all of us together. Sometimes he just talked to us one at a time.

I don't remember much of what Reverend Parks said. I do remember that one time when I was alone with him, he started talking about how there *really was* a God. He said that just because we couldn't see God, it didn't mean that He wasn't with us. Reverend Parks said that we had to have faith, and if we had faith, everything would come to us—everything would be all right.

It kind of puzzled me—not what he said, but the way he said it. It was like he was arguing with me. Like he really didn't think I believed in God and he was trying to convince me.

I thought it was sort of dumb. I mean, I couldn't see the air, but I knew it was there. I could breathe it. I couldn't see the wind—but it was there, too. I could see the way the tree limbs and leaves moved when it pushed them. I could see the grass wiggle and lean over to the side when the wind caressed the long stems. I couldn't see the thoughts in my head, but I knew they were real, too. I could think things—dream. I dreamed that someday Jimmy and I'd go fishing with Daddy. I dreamed about going swimming, or maybe going on vacation this summer to the mountains.

There were lots of things I couldn't see. But they were real. They were there. It didn't make sense for Reverend Parks to try so hard to tell me something I already knew.

When he finished talking with me, he called Jimmy into

his office. I asked Mama and Daddy if I could go into the church.

Mrs. Wineham was practicing the organ pieces for next Sunday. She was a little, white-headed lady. She was kind of old and her face was all wrinkled up like a prune, but she was nice.

She didn't see me when I came in, and I didn't want to bother her. So I snuck back out the door, went down to the basement, and got to the balcony by way of the stairs at the back of the sanctuary.

I sat at the very top of the balcony. It was the highest place in the whole church. I looked at the big, wooden beams that stretched across the chapel. I remembered my little-kid thoughts of the angels sitting there. I looked at the big speaker and thought about God—and I *knew*, even if I couldn't see Him—He was around someplace.

The music from the organ was mellow and sweet. Mrs. Wineham always played well. I didn't recognize the song, but it sure was pretty.

All of a sudden, there was a deep, grumbling sound. Mrs. Wineham kept playing, but the deep note stayed in the air. I could hear it even above her song.

At last she stopped, but the deep, low note that growled from the organ didn't. It just kept going—deeper and louder.

Mrs. Wineham stood up and pounded the top of the organ with her fist. The sound only got louder. Then, that sweet little old lady slugged the organ a couple more times before sitting down and reaching under the keyboard to turn it off.

The low note from the organ was so deep, it made my chest rattle. It died away slowly when she turned the switch on the organ.

Mama walked in about then. Mrs. Wineham looked at her with a smile and shook her head. "If Reverend Parks doesn't hurry up and get the new organ and the new organ pipes installed, I'm gonna go nuts."

Mama smiled back at her. Mrs. Wineham gave the organ a little kick. Then she pointed at the organ pipes.

They were hidden behind a wire-mesh panel at the back of the choir. Through the screen, I could see the big, long pipes that made the low sounds. The pipes tapered down to little, small ones. They were near the center and made the high sounds.

"That bass pipe keeps sticking," she told Mama. "I'll be playing along, hit that low note, then all of a sudden—there she goes. Gets so loud and deep, it feels like an earthquake."

Mama smiled again. "You do a beautiful job of playing the organ."

Mrs. Wineham shrugged. "I try. But if they don't get this thing fixed, it's going to stick during the services one of these days. Sure going to be embarrassing. Wish they'd get the thing fixed."

Mama looked up toward the balcony.

"Nick," she called.

I stood up and waved to her.

"We're through," she said. "We'll meet you in the car."

Mrs. Wineham was right. Next Sunday, with the whole congregation singing "Peace in the Garden," the bass note on the organ got stuck.

She didn't beat the top of the organ though, as she had when she thought there was nobody around. But she did have to turn off the switch. Then we had to start the song over again.

By the end of June, Jimmy quit coming into my room at night to talk. He just went to bed and went to sleep. His visits at the doctor's didn't last as long and he didn't seem as scared as he used to be about going. It was kind of like he didn't much care anymore.

He lost a bunch of weight, too. I didn't even realize that until one day in early July. It was right after the big Fourth of July celebration at Shannon Springs Park when to everybody's surprise Jimmy had started to feel better.

He came running in one afternoon while I was reading a book. He was wearing his pearl-handled six-shooters and his boots. They were on the wrong feet.

"Let's play cowboys," he shouted.

I made him change his boots to the right feet while I went to get my rifle and six-shooter.

We played and ran all over the yard and the neighbor's yard, too. We laughed and giggled and shot each other. When Jimmy took a good shot at me and yelled "BANG," I fell down. He never did.

"You're not playing right," I griped at him. "When I shoot you, you *never* fall down."

He kind of pouted. Then it was my turn to go hide and ambush him. He went to the porch. I hid behind Mrs. Pruitt's lilac bush. When Jimmy came hunting for me, I let him get really close. At the last second, I aimed my rifle, jumped to my feet, and yelled "BANG."

Jimmy looked at me. Then, the pearl-handled six-shooter dropped from his hand. His arms went limp and he plopped to the ground.

I rushed around the lilac bush, whipped out my six-shooter, and blasted him a couple more times, just to make sure.

"BANG! BANG!"

He was flat on the ground with his arms flopped out at his sides. His hat fell off when he went down. I stood there, aiming my pistol down at him.

All of a sudden, my heart jumped up in my throat. He hadn't grabbed his hat, and his bald head was lying on the cold grass. His eyes were closed. He was as still as death.

I put the gun in my holster. "Okay. Your turn to hide."

Jimmy just lay there. He didn't move a muscle.

It was then that I noticed how thin he was. His little arms looked all bony. Even his head was so skinny I could see the sharp lines of his jaws. The blue veins kind of stuck out of his bald head.

My heart seemed to stop. My insides felt real heavy.

He didn't move at all.

"Jimmy," my voice cracked, "Jimmy? Get up."

He still didn't move.

I froze, looking at my little brother. My eyes hurt, straining as I watched him. Then I could see his little skinny tummy move up and down. An eye popped open.

"Did I do it right, Nick?"

He sat up. The air whooshed out of me. My hands started to shake.

Jimmy picked up his pistol and got up.

"Did I do it right?"

I swallowed the big knot in my throat and nodded.

Jimmy took off toward the house.

"You wait on the porch. I get to hide this time."

I shook my head.

"No, Jimmy! I don't want to play anymore!"

I didn't know why I was still shaking so hard. I didn't know why my insides felt turned upside down.

The next time we went to counseling with Reverend Parks, I told him about it. I tried to tell him how it made me feel, but I figured he wouldn't understand.

He did.

"When I was your age," he told me, "we used to play 'army.' We'd pretend one bunch of guys were the good guys and another bunch were the bad guys and we'd try to set ambushes and stuff—have a regular war."

He glanced at the door, like he was making extra sure it was shut.

"Then, when I was eighteen, I went to Vietnam."

"What's Vietnam?" I asked.

"It was what was called a 'Police Action'—but it was really a war. When I got there, I found out that 'army' wasn't play. It wasn't fun. When people got shot, they got hurt or they got killed. That's what real war is like. When people get shot, it hurts, something terrible. Sometimes, when they get shot, they don't get up at all. They don't ever get up—not ever again. They die.

"I think that's what happened with you and Jimmy— when you saw him lying there, and he didn't move. I think you sensed for the first time that he might really die. What do you think?"

I didn't answer Reverend Parks. I didn't think about it. I didn't want to think about it.

CHAPTER
15

I didn't want to think about it, but I guess I should have.

Jimmy got to feeling worse. He got skinnier, too. By the end of July, he had to go back to the hospital. Only this time he didn't get to come home after three or four days.

It was August 12. I guess I'll remember that day for as long as I live.

Jimmy had been really bad sick. He slept almost all the time. In fact, for the past three days, he hadn't been awake at all—not even once.

Last week, Daddy had quit helping with the new Sunday-school building down at the church. Every day, as soon as he got off work, he came and got me and we drove to the city to be with Jimmy and Mama. This week, Daddy quit going to work. We all stayed at the hospital with Jimmy.

He had a private room now instead of a bed in one of the wards. That meant I could visit him, too. There was a little cot in the room. That's where we took turns sleeping. One of us was with him all the time. The only time we weren't there was when we went to the cafeteria to get something to eat—and that was only for a few minutes.

A couple of times I stayed alone with Jimmy when Mama and Daddy went downstairs for coffee or something. I'd talk to him while they were gone. I'd tell him about the mall or about Buck. Only, he never answered. He just lay there with his eyes closed.

I'd get very quiet and watch to see if his chest moved up and down. Sometimes I'd even go over to his bed and lean my ear ever so gently down on his chest. If I saw him breathing or heard his heart beat, it always made me smile. I'd sigh with relief, then sit back down and talk to him some more.

We'd just finished eating that afternoon and were headed back to Jimmy's room. We got off the elevator, and down the hall, I could see a doctor and two nurses coming out of Jimmy's doorway.

"Oh, no," Mama screamed. She took off, running toward them. Daddy and I followed.

At the doorway to Jimmy's room, the doctor grabbed

her. He hugged her tightly to him. Daddy and I raced up behind them. The doctor reached out and held us, too.

"I'm so sorry," he said. "There was nothing we could do. He's gone."

Mama started crying. Daddy hugged both of us, and the doctor, too. Then Mama pulled away and rushed into the room.

Jimmy was lying on the bed. His eyes were closed, but he didn't move. He had had a needle in his arm with a long tube from a jar hooked to it. That was gone, too.

"When," Mama asked the doctor, "when?"

The doctor cleared his throat. "He passed away about ten minutes ago."

Mama let out a moan. It was the loudest, saddest, emptiest, and most helpless sound I'd ever heard in my life. Then she fell across Jimmy and hugged him as hard as she could.

"I didn't want you to be alone when you died," she repeated again and again. "I should have stayed with you. I didn't want you to die alone."

I couldn't stand watching my mama hurt like that. I came up beside her and hugged her.

"He wasn't alone, Mama," I told her. "He wasn't alone."

Mama didn't act as if she'd heard me. But I had to make her hear. I had to tell her that Jimmy wasn't alone.

It was like Reverend Parks had said in one of his sermons . . . "No one is *ever* alone, because God and Jesus are always with us. . . ." And it said the same thing in the

Bible. We'd heard it in Sunday school for as long as I could remember.

I couldn't let Mama hurt like this. I couldn't let her keep thinking that Jimmy was alone.

"He wasn't alone!" I told her again.

But . . . I guess grown-ups don't always listen to little kids. . . .

After a time, Mama let go and quit hugging him. She clung to Daddy and he clung to her. I looked at my little brother. It was like the day we played cowboys.

I watched his chest. It didn't move. And finally, when Mama and Daddy were still crying and holding each other and talking to the doctor—all at the same time—I figured nobody was watching. I snuck over to Jimmy and laid my ear gently against his chest.

There was nothing but silence.

The tears rolled out of my eyes. I hugged him as hard as I could. I kept right on hugging my baby brother until Daddy finally came. He took me by the shoulders and pulled me to him.

Then Mama and Daddy and I hugged and cried— forever.

Three days later, in his little coffin at the front of the church—where the communion table was—Jimmy looked the same way.

His eyes were closed. His hands were crossed over his

chest. The blue veins kind of stuck out on his bald head. He was so skinny and weak-looking. And he didn't move.

As I looked down at the coffin where he lay, I felt as if someone had reached in and torn my heart into little pieces.

Mama knelt beside me and hugged me. Her cheek was wet against mine. She held me really tight, then slowly, she let go.

"Do you want to be alone with him for a moment?" she asked. "Before the funeral starts?"

All I could do was give one little nod of my head.

"I'll be right outside if you need me." She bit her bottom lip and walked away.

I don't know how long I stood there. I held my breath, watching his skinny, little tummy—hoping it would go up and down with his breathing.

It didn't.

I watched, never blinking. But it didn't happen.

His eyes didn't pop open either.

Finally, after a long, long time, I reached over and touched his hands. They were cold. I leaned down and kissed him on the cheek.

His cheek was cold, too. I gently wiped off the place where I had kissed him, because I knew Jimmy didn't like wet, sloppy kisses any more than I did.

"I love you," I whispered.

*   *   *

Then I wheeled around and rushed to where Mama and Daddy were, by the door.

"His hat," I told them. "We've got to get Jimmy's hat from up by the chimney. He wouldn't like all the people at the funeral seeing him without his hat."

Mama shook her head. "He wanted you to have it," she answered. "When he was so sick"—she began to cry— "when he knew he wasn't going to get better, he told me . . ."

She stopped and wiped the tears off her face.

"He told me he wanted you to have his hat. He said something about how he owed it to you . . . something about spurs and a star. It didn't make sense, but he wanted you to have it."

Before, it felt like my insides were all tied in knots. Now—quick as the blink of an eye—I just felt empty, like there was nothing inside me. No hurt. No happy. Just empty.

It was a day or two after Jimmy's funeral when I finally told Mama and Daddy about how I felt. They hugged and kissed me and said I would get better.

"It takes time though, but you'll be better. Just wait and see."

I waited, but after two months, I didn't see that I felt any better.

School had started on August 22. That had helped, I

guess. For a little while each day, I could get busy doing my work or trying to figure out my math paper, and for a second or two, I could forget about Jimmy.

I could forget how much I missed my little brother. But when the bell rang and I went home, my feelings all came crashing back in on me again.

Mama and Daddy tried to help, only I couldn't explain to them what was wrong. We heard on TV that the USA Central Mall was opening in two weeks. They asked if I wanted to go look at it. I didn't.

Daddy tried to get me to ride Buck. Without Jimmy, I didn't want to. Finally, Mama and Daddy gave him to a family who lived in the country. They said he would have a good home.

I missed Buck, but in a way I was glad he was gone because he reminded me of Jimmy—and remembering Jimmy kept the empty feelings I had inside from going away.

Being empty inside hurts after a while.

It was early in November when Mama and Daddy asked the people from the Salvation Army to come. They tried to get me to go through Jimmy's belongings and see if there was anything I wanted to keep. All the rest of his stuff was going to the Salvation Army, where it would be given to needy people.

Going into Jimmy's room—with all the furniture and clothes and the bed made—well . . . it was hard on Mama. So I was glad the men were taking everything away.

It was hard on me, too. That's why when Mama and Daddy asked if there was any of Jimmy's stuff I wanted, I told them no and went in the backyard to play with Poky until the men were gone.

When I heard the truck drive off, I went to my room. There, in the middle of my bed, was Jimmy's Stetson. I knew there was no use arguing with Mama and Daddy—because Jimmy had told them to give it to me. So I picked it up and went outside again.

I walked to the stepladder by the chimney. Some of Mama's dewberry vines had grown around the bottom step and were beginning to crawl toward the second. I climbed the ladder. The Styrofoam head that was nailed to the big board was still there.

I pulled the pins out, stuck Jimmy's hat on the head and pinned it into place. Then I put it back under the eave of the house—where the rain and snow couldn't get to it, where the wind wouldn't blow it away, where the morning dew could touch it and the morning sun could dry the little drops that came from the cold.

I looked up at the sky. My eyes blurred.

"It's your hat," I managed between clenched teeth. "I don't want it. It's yours."

Then I went inside.

CHAPTER
16

School kept getting harder in fifth grade. I had to work! In a way, I liked that. It kept me busy—kept my mind off . . . things. Recess was okay, too—until October. That's when David Beckman and his family moved to Detroit. David and I had been friends ever since kindergarten. We'd always played together at recess. I was sad when he moved away.

Now my brother *and* my best friend were both gone.

School wasn't bad though. I never got in trouble or stuff like that. In fact, the only time I ever got sent to the counselor's office was during music class.

Mrs. Carmine let us play some of the musical instruments one day. She talked to us about them and then went to her closet. She gave most of the boys sticks to clunk together. Two guys had little things like drums. Beth Matlow got a metal thing called a "gong" and four of the other girls got things called "xylophones" that they hit with a stick. Mrs Carmine handed me some tiny bells that were stuck on a red stick.

On my way to my chair, I shook them.

The high, jingling, tinkling sound reminded me of Jimmy's laugh.

When I heard it, the corners of my mouth drooped. I sat down, and when my bottom hit the chair, the bells jingled again. I wrapped my hand around them and held them as hard as I could so they wouldn't jingle.

Everybody took turns playing along with the music on Mrs. Carmine's tape player. But when she pointed to me, I didn't play. I just squeezed the bells tighter. Finally, she stopped the tape. She told me to jingle my bells. I said, "No."

She got that mean "teacher look" on her face and stuck her fists on her hips. "Nick, everyone in class is participating. You will participate also!"

I shook my head.

Her eyes narrowed. "Nick! Play your bells."

"NO."

When her eyebrows went up, her forehead got all wrinkly. "If you refuse to participate, I have no other choice but to send you to the office. Just jingle them."

"NO!"

*   *   *

When I got to the office, Mrs. Easton, the principal, was on the telephone. That didn't surprise me, because Tim Lucas (who got sent to the office a bunch) had told us that Mrs. Easton was always on the phone. He said that she was usually talking to some guy called a superintendent about what a great job she was doing—and didn't have time to mess with us kids.

We figured he knew what he was talking about. I mean, Tim was in trouble and down at the office almost all the time.

Anyway, Mrs. Easton told Mrs. Pfiffer, the secretary, to take me to the counselor.

Mrs. Jones, the counselor, asked me why I wouldn't play the bells for Mrs. Carmine. I didn't feel like telling her the sound reminded me of Jimmy's laugh. I figured it wasn't any of her business.

When I wouldn't talk to her, she opened a big folder with my name on the outside. She flipped through some of the pages. She frowned. "Do you like music?"

I shrugged.

"Do you like Mrs. Carmine?"

I shrugged.

She read some more. "Is it the song that you didn't like or the noise or . . . oh . . . goodness."

She peeked over the top of the folder with one eye. "Does it have something to do with . . . ah . . . your brother?"

I didn't answer. I just folded my arms and sat there.

She asked a bunch more questions but I didn't feel like answering. Finally, when music class was over, she let me go back to my room. Next time I went to music, Mrs. Carmine didn't make me play any of the instruments.

At school, I worked hard. I went out for recess and ran and played soccer or climbed around on the playground stuff. I laughed with the other guys and we chased the girls sometimes.

At home, I worked on homework. I played my Nintendo (everything except Contra, because that was one of Jimmy's favorites).

At night, I thought about Jimmy. I thought about playing cowboys. I thought about that ugly hat that he loved so much. I thought about how lonely it was without him. And I wished he could come back.

And I knew the empty feeling would never go away.

We went to counseling at the church. It didn't seem to help. We went to the Wichita Mountains and drove around and looked at the buffalo and stuff. Sometimes at night I would think about the buffalo and the mountains. But memories of Jimmy would always creep in and I'd remember how much I missed him.

I didn't go trick-or-treating at Halloween. Thanksgiving sort of came and went without much notice.

There was a lot of stuff about the USA Central Mall on the TV. One day on the screen, I saw a new statue at the Cowboy Hall of Fame. I saw Mr. Scott. He was talking with some guys, and I recognized him by his rumpled hat and the way his tummy stuck out over his big belt buckle.

Watching TV had always been a good way to keep from thinking about my brother. I could sit for hours and watch and keep my mind off him.

When I saw Mr. Scott—well, I liked seeing him again— but it hurt, too. It reminded me of Jimmy and all the fun we had had that day at the Cowboy Hall of Fame.

Thinking about Jimmy made me hurt. It made me mad, too. It wasn't fair for a neat little kid like him to have to die!

I guess I stayed mad for quite a while. And finally, when the hurt and the mad went away, I just felt kind of empty again. It was the same empty that I felt the day I kissed my brother on the cheek before the funeral. Empty hurts.

So, instead of watching TV and seeing stuff about the mall or maybe seeing Mr. Scott again, I started reading. Reading turned out to be even better than watching TV. I could spend hours in my room. I went places, I had adventures. I even felt myself smile a few times.

Mrs. Timms, our librarian at school, helped me find lots of neat stuff to read. I told her that I didn't want any sad books though, and she always got me good ones. She gave me *Charlie Drives the Stage* by Eric Kimmel, and *Judge Benjamin: Superdog* by Judith McInerney. She gave me two books by a guy called Thomas Rockwell. One was called *How to Fight a Girl*. The other was titled *How to Eat Fried Worms*. Each time I went to the library, Mrs. Timms had another neat book for me.

When I wasn't reading, I tried to make myself think about the Christmas tree at church.

Reverend Parks told us about it last Sunday. Before the sermon, he always told about the Ladies' Club meetings or about Church League Softball or stuff that happened in the business meeting.

Usually it was boring. But when he started talking about the tree, my ears perked up. He said that the tree we were going to have in our sanctuary was going to be a cedar tree. He said that it would have no lights or store-bought ornaments on it.

Our tree would be very special this year. It would be decorated with handmade stuff. There would be snowflakes that the Ladies' Club would make out of lace. There would be popcorn strings and cranberry strings that we would make in Sunday-school class. "And most important," he'd said, "things that the children bring from home, things that they make themselves or something they've found that is very special to them and that they want to share with others.

"Our tree will be old-fashioned. It won't be decorated with bright lights or fancy bulbs. It will be decorated with gifts from our hearts, because gifts from our hearts are what Christmas is *really* about."

So when I wasn't reading, I tried to figure what I could make or what I could find (maybe in my toy box or something) that would be special enough for our church tree.

Only I couldn't think of anything.

CHAPTER
17

The Saturday before Christmas Sunday, I still hadn't thought of a single thing for the tree.

I finally gave up.

I got up Saturday morning to fix some chocolate milk. Mama and Daddy got up right after I did. They drank their coffee in the kitchen. I heard Daddy say he was going down to the church. The new speakers that he and the other men had worked on getting for so long had finally arrived. They were going to put them up, then do some painting. He told Mama it would probably be late tonight before he got home.

Since Jimmy died, it seemed like Daddy worked late a bunch. He was either at the office or helping down at the church.

Maybe work, for Daddy, was like school for me. Maybe it helped keep his head busy.

Mama was just as bad. She went back to teaching and stayed late to grade papers or get her room ready. When she got home, she cleaned. She washed dishes. She swept the floor. She was always dusting something.

I once thought that if I had been a grown-up, it wouldn't have hurt so much when Jimmy died. Then I decided that being a grown-up wouldn't help at all. When you lose somebody you love, I guess it hurts—no matter how old you are.

Mama got some Comet and cleaned the sinks when Daddy left. I watched Bugs Bunny.

When the cartoons were over and those dumb little news programs started, I went into my bedroom to finish the book I had started. I heard Mama turn the TV back on when it was time for the news and weather. When the news was over, she came in and dusted my room.

"Weatherman said a cold front's coming," she said. "It's a big one and they're predicting sleet and snow."

I looked up over the top of my book.

"The cold front's supposed to hit sometime tonight or early Sunday," she said, dusting my soccer trophy. "If it's as bad as they say, Poky will have to come inside for a few days." She put my trophy down and dusted the mirror. "Why don't you go give him a bath? He hasn't had a bath since school started, and I don't want him stinking up the house."

I grunted and put my bookmark on the page I was reading.

There was a big, silver tub hanging on the wall in the garage. I took it down and filled it with warm water from the tap beside the washer. I got Poky's flea soap down from the shelf and put some of that in, too. Then I went out in the backyard.

How Poky knew I was planning to give him a bath, I don't know. Maybe he heard the water running in the tub. Maybe he smelled the flea soap. Whatever . . . he always seemed to know when it was bath time.

I called him. He wagged his tail and started toward me, then stopped dead in his tracks. He gave me a funny look and took off for the far side of the yard.

I called him again, and when he didn't come, I went after him. That crazy dog ran all over the yard. I chased him round and round. He let me get almost close enough to get my hands on him, then took off again.

Once, I tried a flying tackle—like I'd seen on Monday Night Football. I missed though, and ended up bumping my head on the chain link fence.

I started after Poky again. I almost got him cornered at the side of the house, but he darted between my legs and made it into his doghouse. I chased him and blocked the doorway so he couldn't get out.

"Got you now, you little stinker," I said.

I stuck my head in. He was way in the back corner. I reached for him, but my shoulders got stuck in the opening. When I was little, I used to crawl in and out of Poky's doghouse without any problem. I guess I'd grown some.

I got myself unstuck, looked at where he was, and decided if I reached in with one hand I could get hold of his leg and drag him out.

When I reached, he scooted back farther into the corner. I took aim again, leaned my cheek against the doorway, and reached as far as I could. And just as I got hold of his leg, a flash of gold caught my eye.

It was so close, I couldn't tell what it was. My cheek was smushed up against the doghouse, and the gold thing was right there by my eyeball. I let go of Poky's leg and leaned back.

There, stuck in a crack at the doorway, was a small, pointy gold star. Somehow, it must have slipped in this crack and got stuck. I squinted, making sure that that's *really* what it was. Then, with my fingertips, I reached in and pulled it out. I held it up to the light.

It was the little star from the end of my spurs—the spurs that Jimmy had broken and worried so much about. The little star that had fallen off, so long long ago, last Christmas.

CHAPTER
18

Daddy got home late that night. I was still awake when he came in. I tiptoed down the hall and leaned my ear close to Mama and Daddy's door. I heard him tell Mama that they had just finished painting the front of the sanctuary. He said the paint would still be wet for the Christmas services, but the new speakers were up and working, and even if the paint was wet, the church would be pretty for Christmas morning.

That's all they talked about.

Mama and Daddy didn't seem to talk much anymore. They didn't talk. They didn't laugh. They didn't even fight—or "have discussions" like they used to.

It was kind of sad.

I went back to my room. I waited and waited and waited.

When I was sure they were asleep, I snuck down the hall to the kitchen. I went out in the backyard. It was really warm for this time of year, but the ground was kind of cold. The dry grass tickled my bare feet.

Careful not to step on the dewberry thorns, I put my foot on the second rung of the stepladder and climbed up. Jimmy's hat was still pinned to the Styrofoam head.

"I found it," I whispered. "It was right at Poky's doghouse. Just like you said it was. It was wedged in one of the cracks by the doorway, that's why we couldn't find it last year. But I found it now."

I looked at the hat. I looked at the way the moonlight filtered through the tree branches.

"Remember how bad you felt about breaking my spurs? Remember how you wanted me to have your hat to make up for it? I told you then that they were just cheap little toy spurs and I didn't care. Only you felt so bad about breaking them, I guess you didn't listen.

"Well, I found it. I fixed the spur, too. All I had to do was stick the star back on it and use Daddy's pliers to squeeze it into place. See?"

I took the spurs from behind my back and laid them beside Jimmy's cowboy hat.

"See? Good as new."

I stood there on top of the ladder for a long time. I looked at Jimmy's hat. I looked at the way the rays of moonlight caught the tip of the little gold star on the spurs.

It was quiet and still. There was no breeze to stir the

bare tree limbs. Just me and Jimmy's hat and the spurs. For some reason, though, I didn't feel lonely. I didn't feel quite as empty as before.

"I know what I'm gonna do with the spurs," I said. "I'm not gonna tell Mama and Daddy or anybody. It's just between you and me."

A bright star seemed to wink at me from above. I winked back. "Just between us," I repeated.

From up here in the balcony, our church's tree looked like the grandest tree in the world. I knew the decorations weren't nearly as expensive as the ones on the trees at some of the stores or malls in Chickasha or in Oklahoma City.

But our little tree was special.

It had all sorts of decorations on it. There were white snowflakes made out of lace. There were strings of popcorn and cranberries. There were old things and new things that sparkled. And on one of the lower branches—tied on with the plastic heel-straps—was a little pair of gold-colored tin spurs.

They swayed and bounced in the gentle breeze that came from the open windows.

It made the tree special—at least to me.

The opening hymn this Christmas Sunday was kind of different. Usually, we sang regular Christmas songs out of our hymnals. Today, we sang "Jesus Loves the Little Children."

It was one I could sing without even looking at the words

in the book. I'd known that song since I was a little kid.

As soon as we were through singing, Reverend Parks came to the podium. With the sleeve of his robe, he wiped the sweat from his forehead.

"Ladies and gentlemen," he said, "I want to apologize for the heat. It's all my fault. When we finished painting the front of the sanctuary last night, I remembered that a cold front was coming. So I turned the heat way up. This morning I heard on the weather report that the front wouldn't be through until noon or so—but I never thought about coming down to turn the heat off."

He motioned with a wave of his hand at the windows. "Our deacons have opened up the sanctuary. That should help." Then he kind of chuckled. "This is typical Oklahoma weather, I guess. It's Christmas Sunday and almost eighty degrees outside."

The assistant preacher read a Scripture next. Then Reverend Parks read one. Then we sang "Silent Night." After we finished singing, Reverend Parks read some of the announcements that were printed in the back of the church program.

Next, he started calling people's names and asked them to stand up. Daddy's was one of the first names he called.

From the back of the balcony, I could see the front of the church okay, but I couldn't see the people sitting down. I had to lean forward in my chair to see Daddy.

Reverend Parks made the people stand even after he was through calling names.

"These men and women are the volunteers who have

been working on the new Sunday-school rooms. Last night, they stayed until midnight installing our brand-new speaker system. Now," he said smiling, "I'd like everyone in the congregation to look up. We have six new speakers which have been carefully hung from the beams at the top of the church."

I had to lean over to see under the rafters. There were six speakers dangling beneath the beams. They were sort of small. I sat up straight and looked down at our preacher. He turned toward where Mrs. Wineham was sitting at the organ.

"Our next project is a new organ for the sanctuary." He smiled at her. "Give us a couple more months and we won't have to worry about the pipes sticking."

Mrs. Wineham smiled back—only her smile wasn't as nice as Reverend Parks's.

The people who had been standing started to sit down.

"Oh," he added, before they were all seated, "I almost forgot. These people also painted the front of the sanctuary last night." He pointed above him. "When we took the old speaker down, there was an unsightly, bare spot. So we decided to paint the whole area instead of trying to match the paint."

I looked up to where he was pointing.

When I did, I jumped. My whole body gave a little jerk. The old, wooden seat in the balcony squeaked.

The big, brown speaker box at the front of the church . . .

It was gone.

I hadn't even noticed before.

There was nothing there. Just a bare wall—a bare wall that shined a little because the paint was still wet.

A horrible thought got hold of me then. A thought that I couldn't get rid of. It made my insides feel even more empty than the day my brother died.

It was a little-kid thought—the thought that being way up high, here in the balcony, somehow let me be closer to God. And I remembered all the times I had looked at the beams across the church and thought about the angels sitting there. And all the times I had looked at that big, brown speaker with the cloth covering and thought that, if God was here, that's where He probably sat.

I knew it was a dumb idea, but I couldn't seem to shake it, no matter what.

My brother died and left me, I thought. My best friend moved to Detroit and left me.

And now—even God has gone off and left me.

A sadness swept over me like a cloud. It made me shiver. My insides were so empty that I couldn't even feel the hurt of being empty. It was like there was nothing left. Nothing at all.

CHAPTER

19

I guess I've always been afraid of being left alone. Maybe lots of people are.

But I never was alone. I mean, there was always David and his family, or Jimmy or Mama and Daddy.

Now, for the first time, I felt all alone.

I didn't like the feeling.

I drew my feet up in the chair underneath me. I wrapped my arms around my legs and hugged my heels in tight against my bottom. The tears started leaking from my eyes. I buried my face against my knees.

By the time we were ready to sing our last hymn, "Oh Come All Ye Faithful," I had quit crying. I didn't quit because I felt any better. I quit because I knew this was our last song and I was going to have to go downstairs. I didn't want anybody to see me crying.

I knew the words to the hymn, at least to most of the first verse, and I figured singing the words might help get rid of the jerking that my insides kept doing. So, I took a deep breath.

"Oh Come All Ye Faithful," I sang, "Joyful and triumphant. Oh come ye, oh come ye to Bethlehem. Come and Behold Him, born the King of Angels . . ."

That's when it happened.

The bass note on Mrs. Wineham's organ got stuck.

It was soft at first, just kind of a low rumble. Reverend Parks glanced at her. Mrs. Wineham held both hands up, as if telling him that she hadn't even touched the thing.

The big, deep sound got louder.

Mrs. Wineham patted the top of the organ. The sound only grew and grew. She smiled sheepishly, then clunked the organ a couple of times with her fist.

Now the low rumbling was so loud it felt as if the whole room were beginning to shake. Quickly, Mrs. Wineham reached down and flipped the switch.

But . . .

Nothing happened. The deep, low, rumbling sound from the bass pipe in the organ just kept getting louder.

Suddenly, I noticed the church programs stacked along the ledge at the windows. They began to flutter, pushed by a sudden wind from outside. A few of them flew off the windowsill. Then, more and more. I leaned forward so I could see over the edge of the balcony.

Some of the old ladies who sat in the pews near the front of the church grabbed their sweaters and wrapped them around their shoulders. It didn't take long to figure out that the cold front mentioned on the news was moving through.

Nobody had heard the wind shift. Nobody had heard the rustling of the leaves on the trees outside because the stuck note on the organ was too loud. More church programs fluttered from the windowsills and went scampering across the room. Some leaves and an old paper bag floated in from outside.

The deacons, who were close to the windows, leaped up and started closing them. They slapped their hands on the little piles of church programs so no more would go fluttering to the floor.

Before they had all the windows closed, the limbs on the Christmas tree started to sway. They flopped and waved back and forth. Reverend Parks ran down from behind his podium to steady the tree. A couple of the lace snowflakes fell to the floor. One of the cranberry strings came loose and draped around Reverend Parks's shoulders.

As the deacons closed the windows, the big, deep sound grew even louder. The yellow stained-glass windows shook. Even the walls quivered and trembled. I put a hand to my chest, feeling the rumbling clear down into my heart. Mrs. Wineham slugged the organ a couple more times. Then she stood up and reached around behind it for the electric plug.

But just as she reached for it, the deep, loud, rumbling sound died away. A puzzled frown was on her face when she sat back down.

A hush fell over our little congregation. The loud, deep sound from the organ had stopped. All the windows had been closed. The people in the pews didn't talk or even wiggle. It was like they were afraid the loud sound would start again or the wind would blow.

There was nothing but stillness.

Finally, Reverend Parks let go of the tree.

With the windows closed, everything had calmed down. The programs didn't flutter across the floor. The tree didn't shake and flop around.

Reverend Parks took the cranberry string that had fallen around his shoulders and draped it back over the tree limb. Then he peeked around the tree. Frowning, he cocked his head to the side, studying the only thing in the whole entire church that was still moving.

One of the tree limbs waved up and down, as if still pushed by some unseen wind. It was a bottom limb on the far side of the tree. Reverend Parks walked around the tree for a closer look. The limb flopped to and fro. He glanced behind him, making sure one of the windows wasn't open. Then he leaned closer to the limb. He frowned curiously at the ornament on the tip of the bouncing branch.

The ornament was a pair of toy cowboy spurs.

As they wiggled and swayed and shook on the end of the limb—another sound came.

It was a high, tinkling sound.

It was a sound like tiny bells jingling inside a tin bucket.

It was a sound like . . .

. . . like Jimmy's laugh.

I never had chill bumps on my heart before.

I'd had chill bumps on my arms. I'd had chill bumps on my tummy and my legs and my back. I had felt the little bumps pop out on my skin. I had felt the hair on my legs like it was tingling and wiggling all over. But I'd never felt chill bumps on my heart.

It was a tingly, exciting feeling at first. Then it was like my breath was all taken away and my heart stopped. Then . . .

Then it felt like one of the hugs that my little brother used to give. Only this time, instead of Jimmy hugging *me*—it was like he had reached clear inside and hugged my very heart.

I shivered. A tear slipped out of my left eye. And at that very same instant, I heard myself laugh. It was the first time I had laughed in a long, long time.

The tinkling, jingling sound stopped just before Reverend Parks reached out to stop the limb from moving. He tilted his head to the other side.

Our church was very, very quiet. In fact, the only sound in the whole church was the sound of my giggling.

Reverend Parks looked up at the balcony. So did Mrs. Wineham. So did the choir.

I slapped a hand over my mouth and got quiet.

Only—my insides laughed and cried and laughed all at the same time.

On the way home, Mama and Daddy said something about how it wasn't like me to make fun of people when something bad happened to them. I told them I wasn't laughing at something bad that happened. I told them I was laughing at something good.

Daddy looked a little puzzled, but he didn't say anymore. Neither did I.

I never told them about going out in the backyard and climbing the ladder beside the chimney. Even though a strong wind had come in with the cold front, the Styrofoam head was still beneath the eave of the house.

But Jimmy's hat was gone!

I remembered our Sunday-school teacher talking about miracles. I remembered how she'd said they didn't have to be big and dramatic, like the Red Sea parting or the big flood. Sometimes there were little miracles. And they were okay, too.

I remembered the day Jimmy died and how upset Mama was because he was all alone. I remembered telling her that Jimmy wasn't alone.

How could I have ever forgotten something so simple?

The Sunday after Christmas, I rocked back in my chair in the balcony. I looked out at the wooden beams that stretched across to support the roof—the wooden beams where the angels sat. I looked down at the toy cowboy spurs in my hand. With my finger, I touched the tip of the little star and gave it a spin. No sound came from it—none at all as the little tin star whirled around.

I folded my arms and looked up to where the big brown speaker box used to be.

I used to think God sat on that old speaker box. I guess God's big enough and strong enough that He doesn't have to have a place to sit. He can be wherever He wants to.

I smiled again.

It was a big, warm, happy smile, the biggest and happiest I could remember since Jimmy died.

Even if Reverend Parks didn't know—even if Mama and Daddy and the rest of the congregation didn't know—I knew.

Jimmy was safe. Nobody could see him, but God really was here. And, He'd let Jimmy come with Him, on Christmas Sunday.

Now, Jimmy had his hat—he wasn't bald while he was waiting for his hair to grow back.

Leaning forward, I looked down at our little congregation. While I watched, Daddy glanced over his shoulder and saw me peeking at him from the balcony.

I put my finger and thumb to my mouth, making a motion like I was zipping my mouth shut. (I'd had to promise Mama and Daddy that I wouldn't laugh anymore if they let me sit in the balcony.)

Daddy nodded. For a moment, he looked a bit puzzled, then he turned back to listen to Reverend Parks.

"How come you want to sit in the balcony, all alone?" Daddy'd wondered when I asked if I could sit here.

I'd reached around him and Mama, both. I'd hugged them as hard as I could. And with a soft smile, I'd told them simply:

"I won't be alone."

ABOUT THE AUTHOR

BILL WALLACE was a principal and physical education teacher at an elementary school in Chickasha, Oklahoma, for ten years. Recently, he has spent much of his spare time assisting his wife in coaching a girls' soccer team. When Bill's not busy on the soccer field, he spends time with his family, cares for his five dogs, three cats, and two horses, lectures at schools around the country, answers mail from his readers, and of course, works on his books. Bill Wallace's novels have won nineteen state awards and made the master lists in twenty-four states.

BILL WALLACE

Award-winning author Bill Wallace brings you fun-filled stories of animals full of humor and exciting adventures.